Phoebe and Her Unicorn in

D0027718

Phoebe and Her Unicorn in The Magic Storm

Dana Simpson

Andrews McMeel
PUBLISHING®

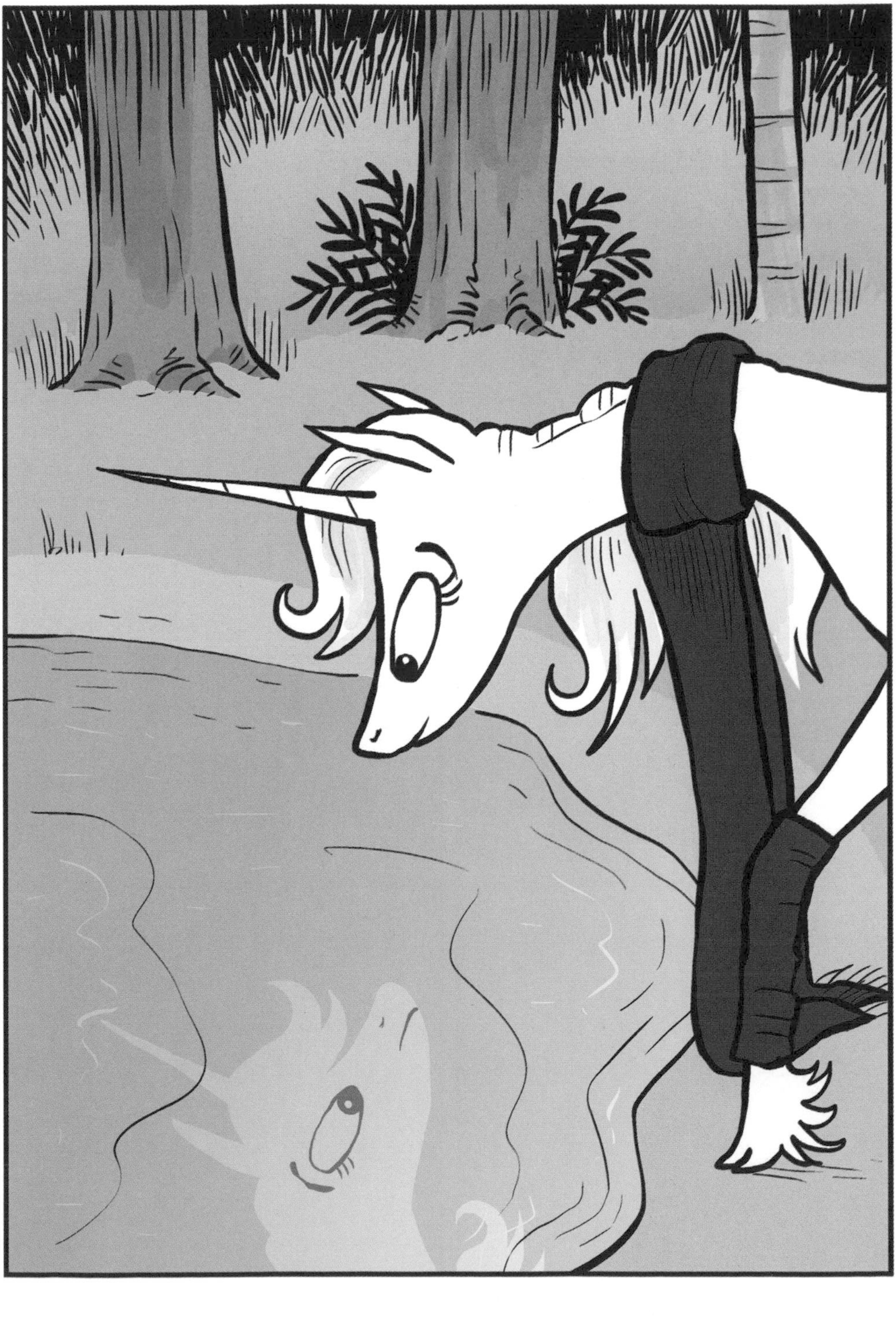

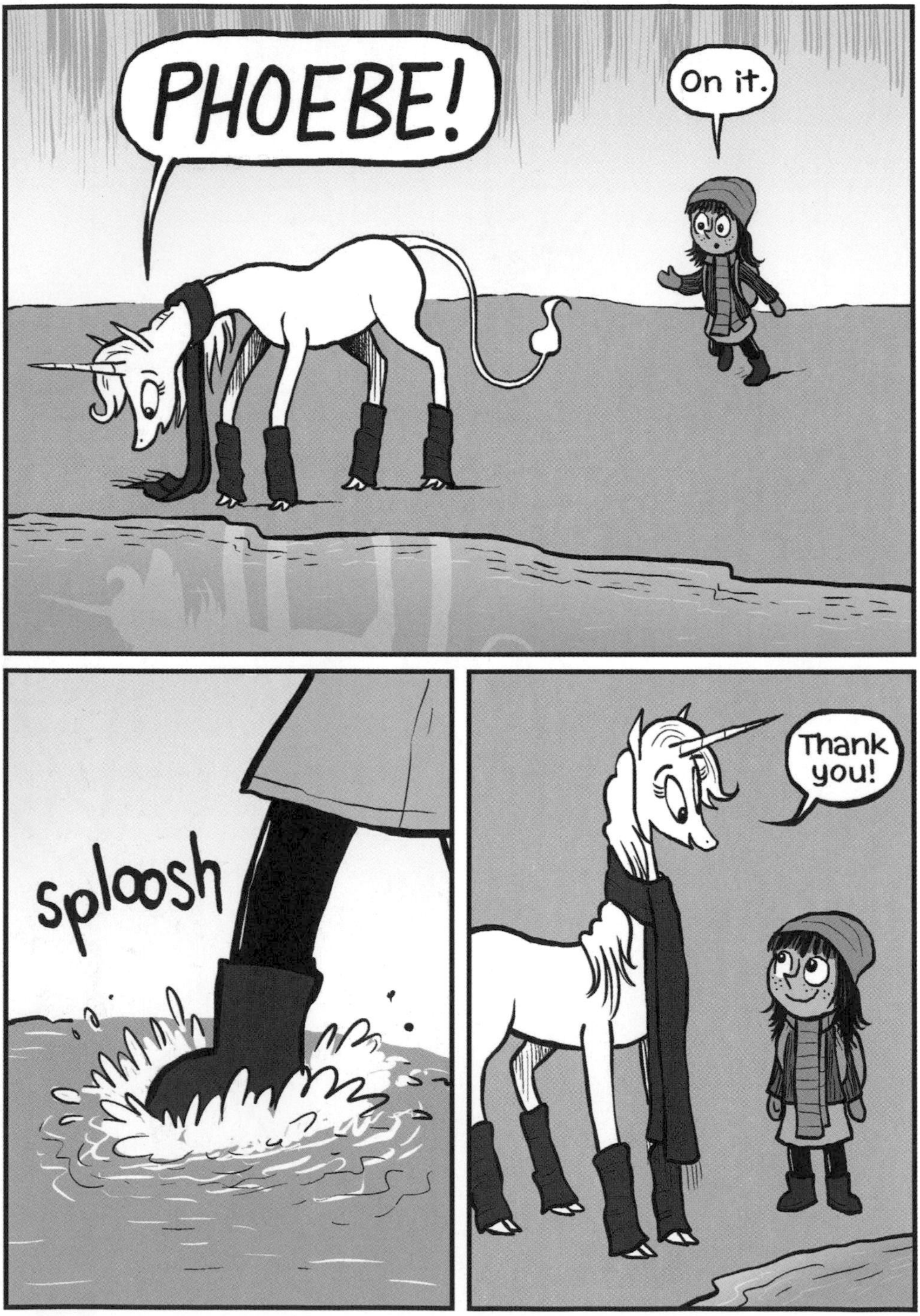
PHOEBE!
On it.
sploosh
Thank you!

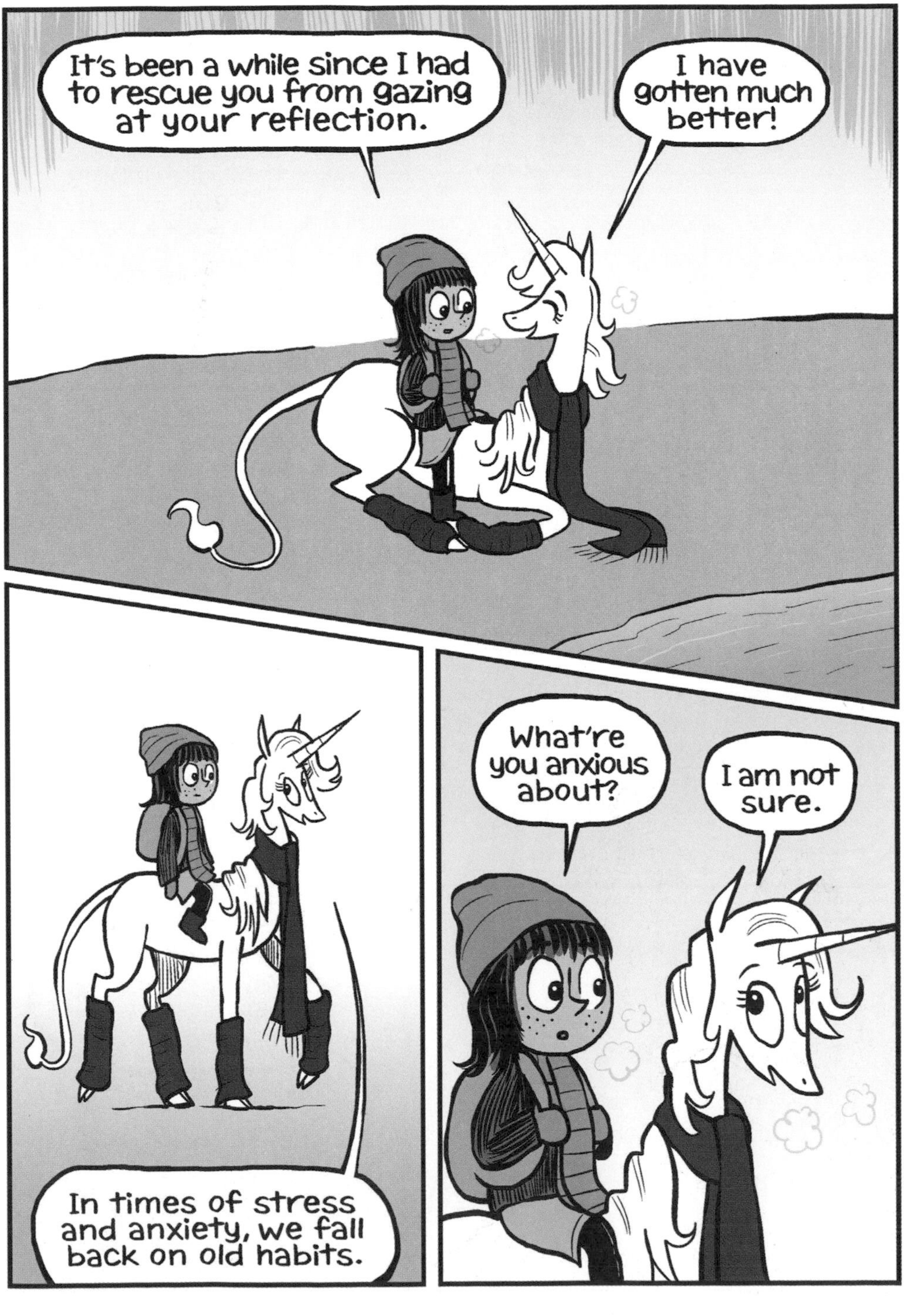
It's been a while since I had to rescue you from gazing at your reflection.
I have gotten much better!
In times of stress and anxiety, we fall back on old habits.
What're you anxious about?
I am not sure.

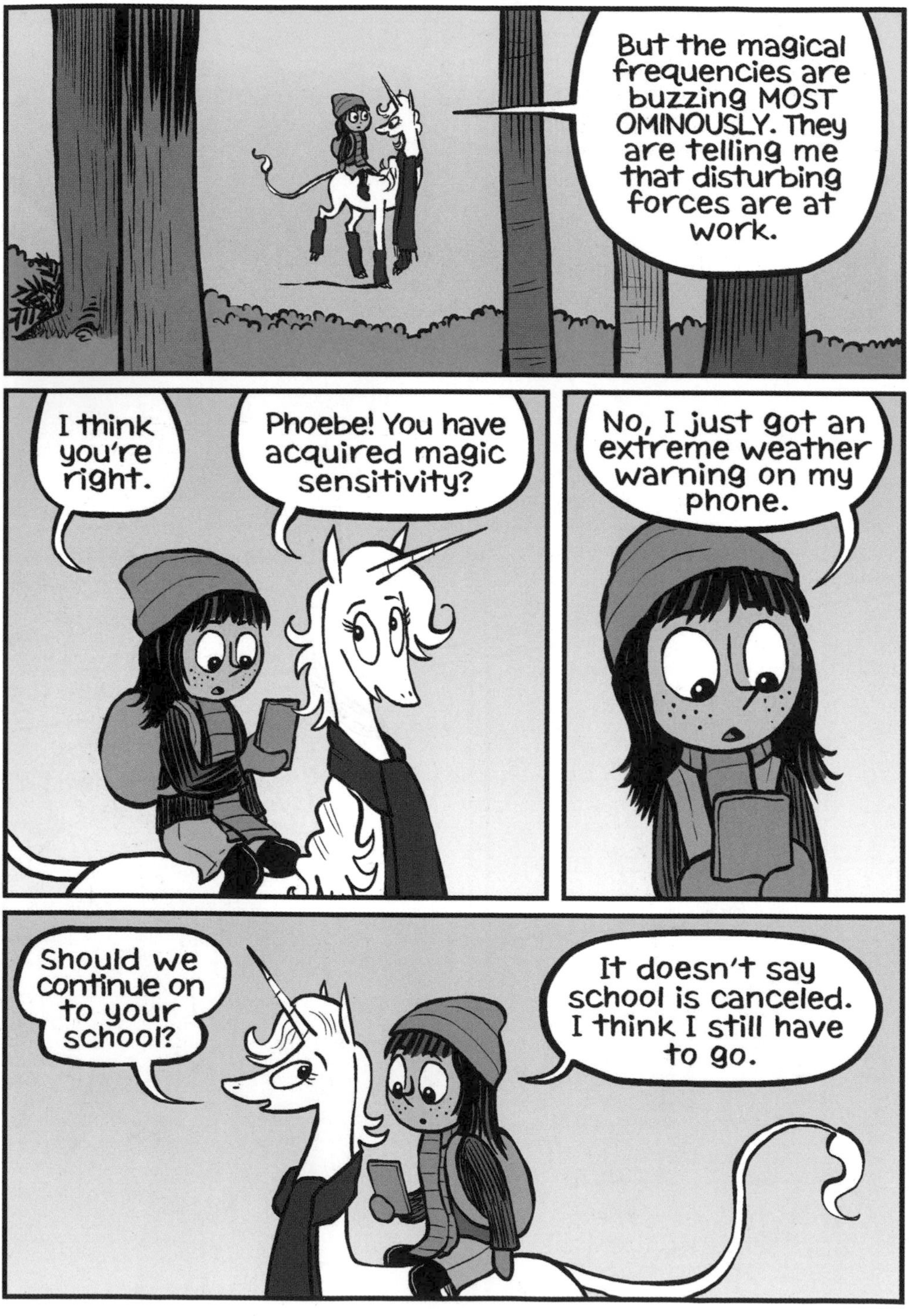
But the magical frequencies are buzzing MOST OMINOUSLY. They are telling me that disturbing forces are at work.
I think you're right.
Phoebe! You have acquired magic sensitivity?
No, I just got an extreme weather warning on my phone.
Should we continue on to your school?
It doesn't say school is canceled. I think I still have to go.

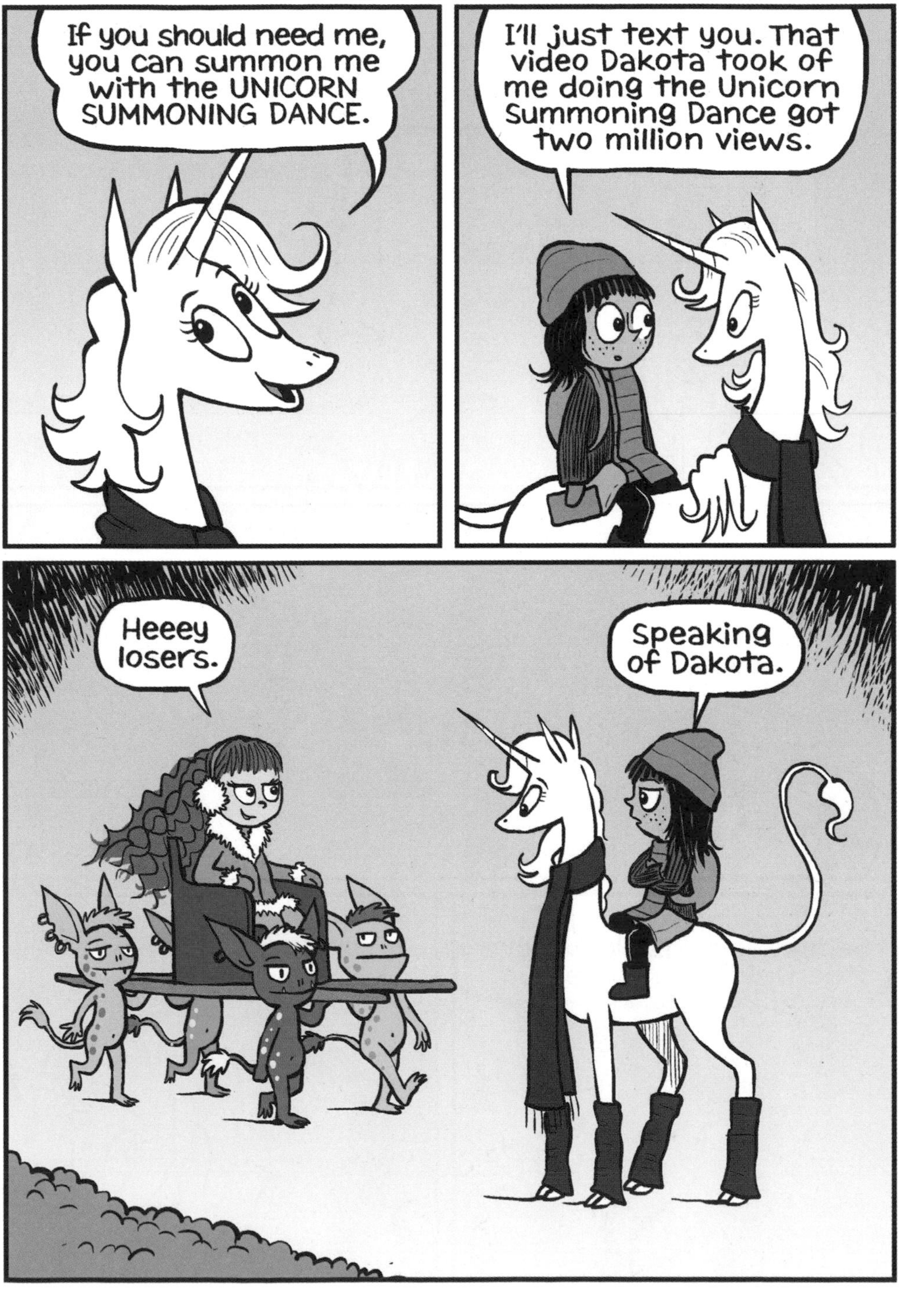
If you should need me, you can summon me with the UNICORN SUMMONING DANCE.
I'll just text you. That video Dakota took of me doing the Unicorn Summoning Dance got two million views.
Heeey losers.
Speaking of Dakota.

How come you still call me that? I ride a UNICORN to school now.
And I actually AM a unicorn.
I think you're JEALOUS.
Of YOU? For THAT? Psh.
I was making fun of you for being a loser LONG before the unicorn showed up.
You were...jealous for some other reason, then!

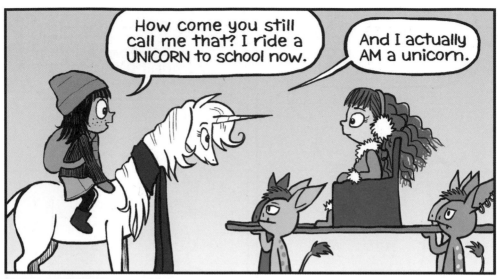

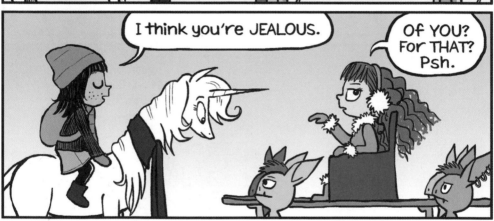

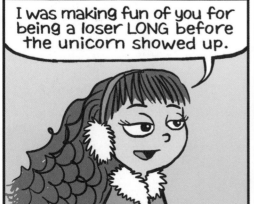

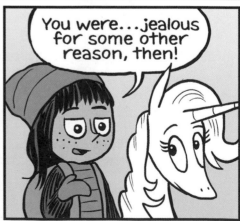

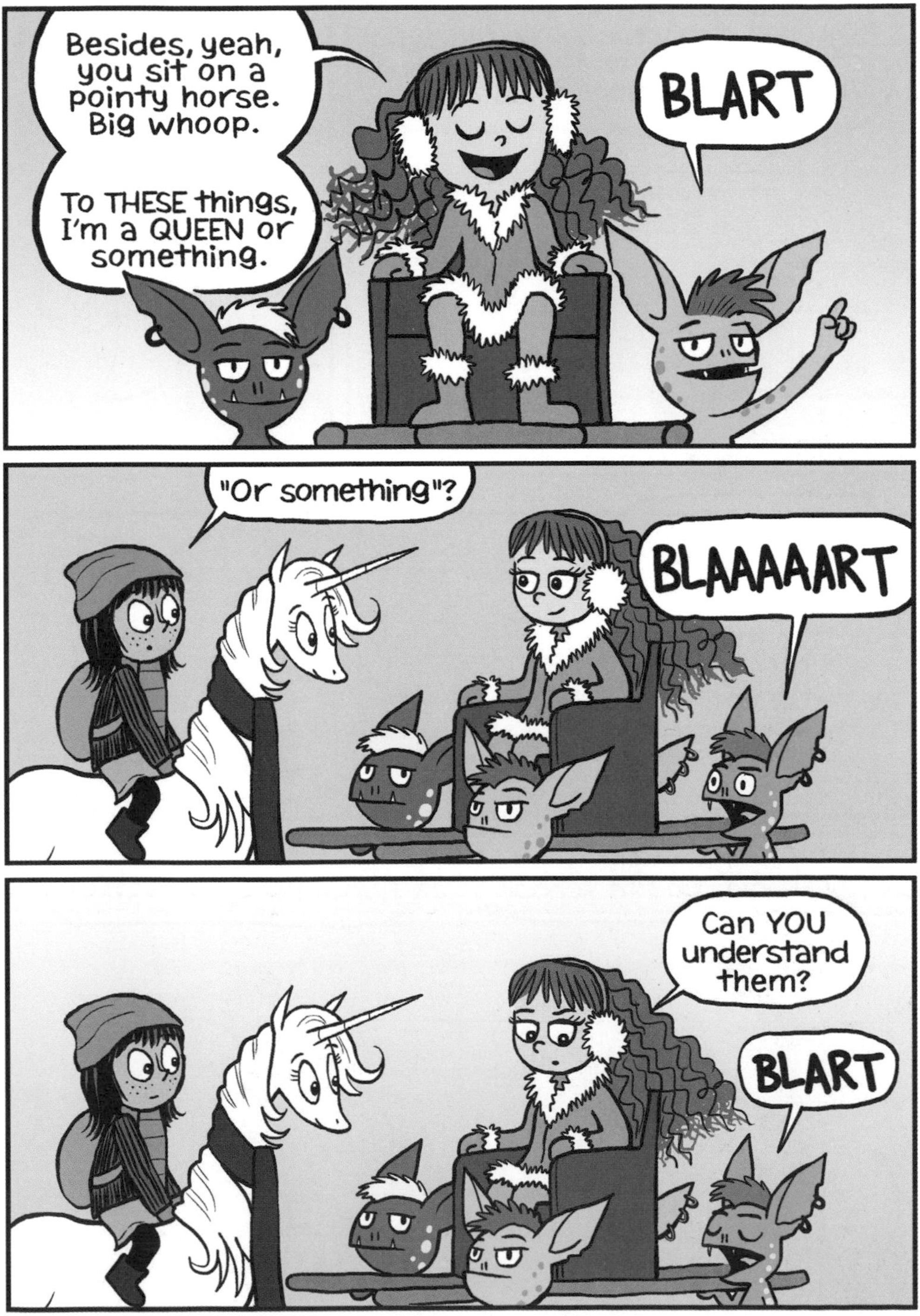
Besides, yeah, you sit on a pointy horse. Big whoop.
TO THESE things, I'm a QUEEN or something.
BLART
"Or something"?
BLAAAAART
Can YOU understand them?
BLART

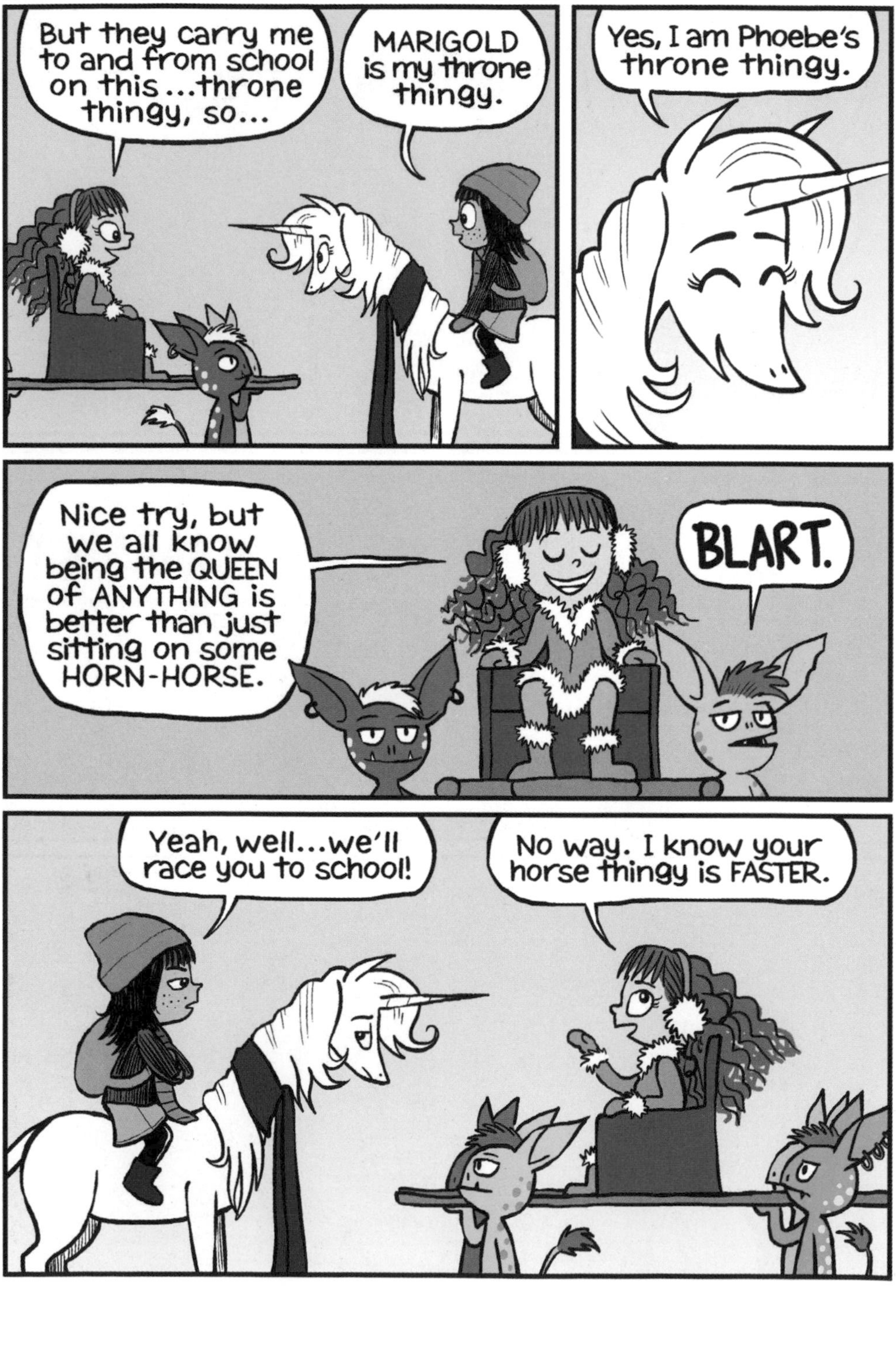
But they carry me to and from school on this...throne thingy, so...
MARIGOLD is my throne thingy.
Yes, I am Phoebe's throne thingy.
Nice try, but we all know being the QUEEN of ANYTHING is better than just sitting on some HORN-HORSE.
BLART.
Yeah, well...we'll race you to school!
No way. I know your horse thingy is FASTER.

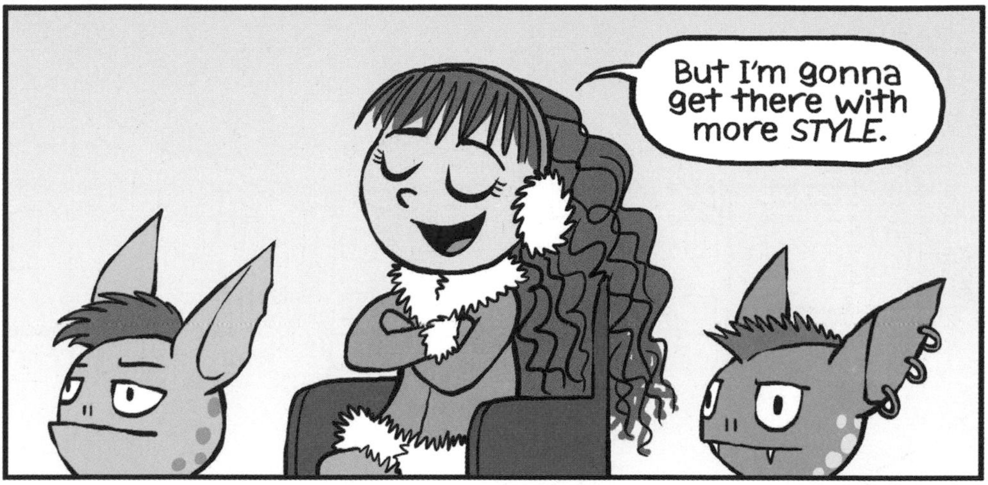
But I'm gonna get there with more *STYLE*.

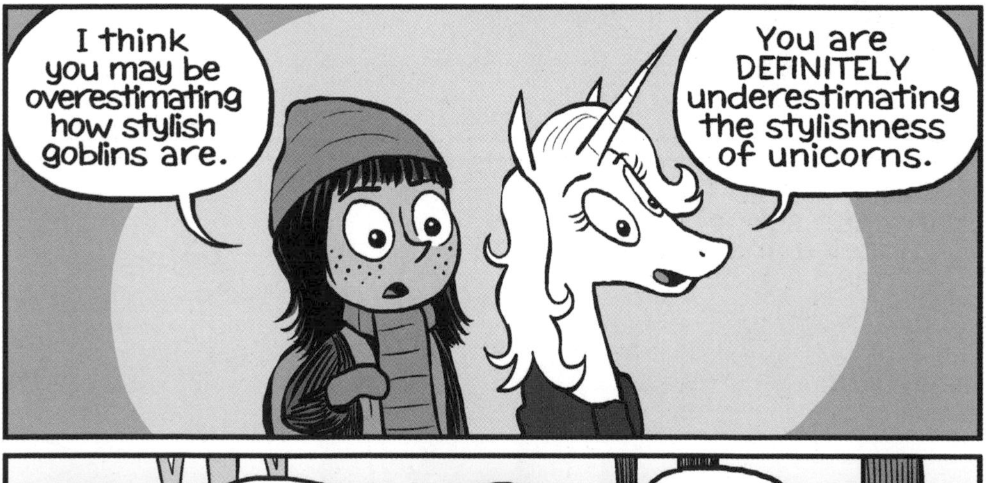
I think you may be overestimating how stylish goblins are.
You are DEFINITELY underestimating the stylishness of unicorns.

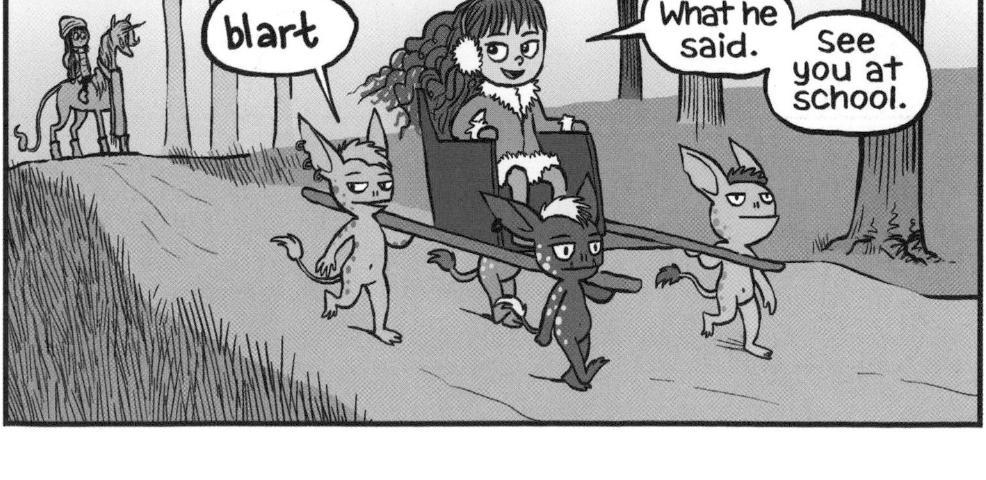
blart
What he said.
See you at school.

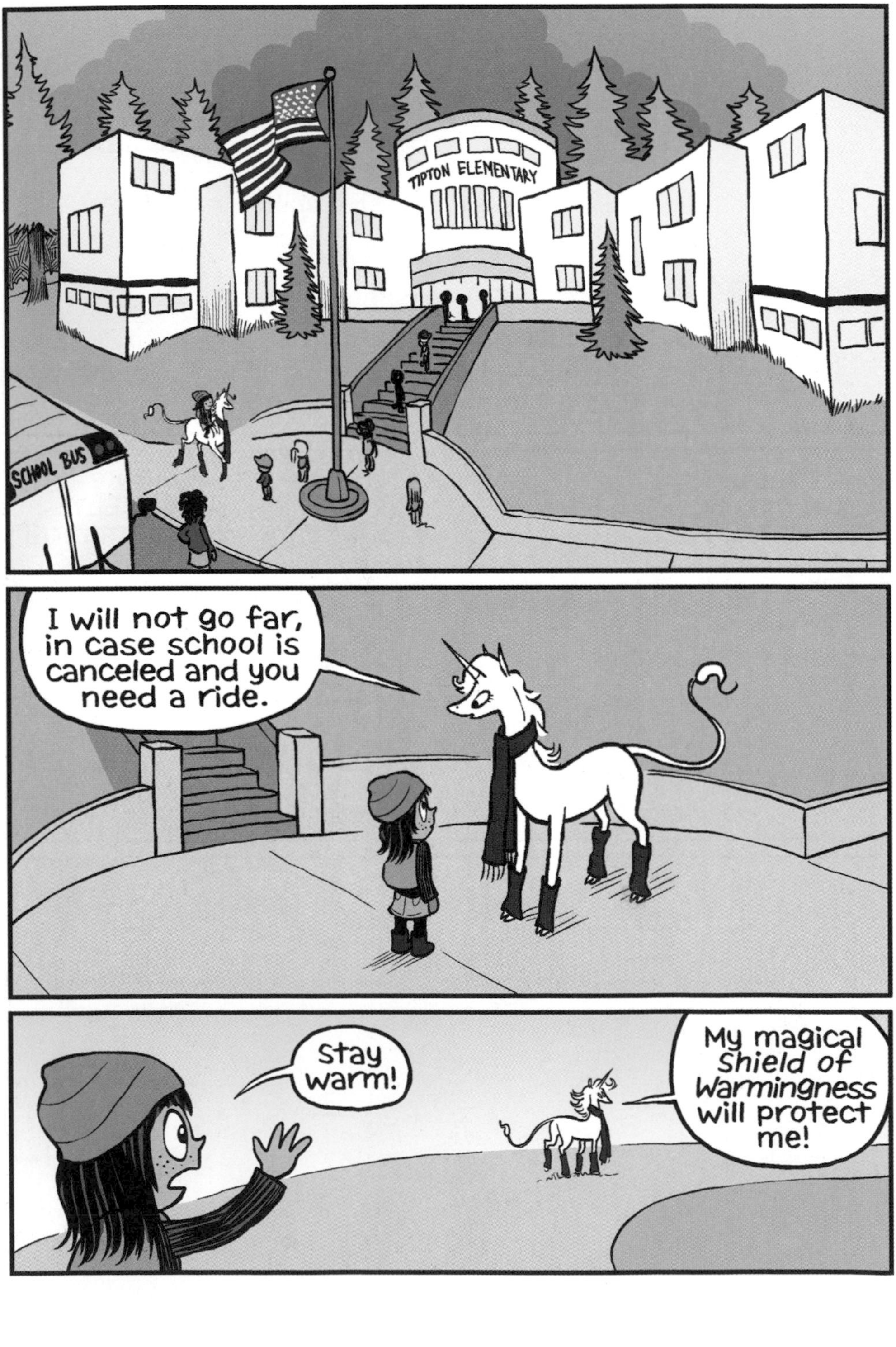
TIPTON ELEMENTARY
SCHOOL BUS
I will not go far, in case school is canceled and you need a ride.
Stay warm!
My magical Shield of Warmingness will protect me!

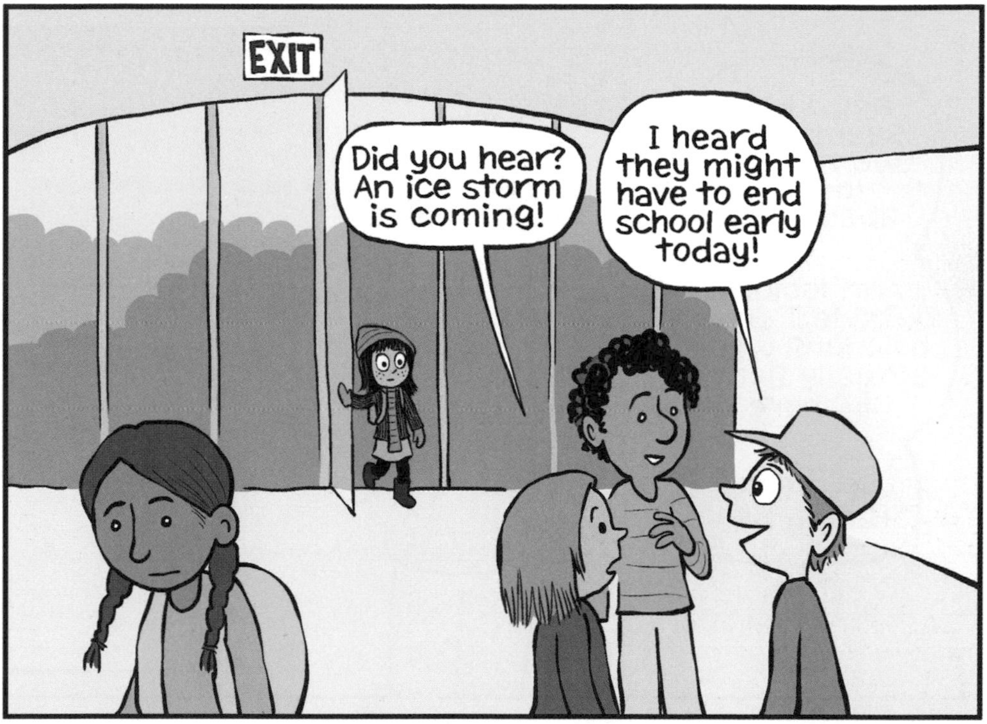
EXIT
Did you hear? An ice storm is coming!
I heard they might have to end school early today!

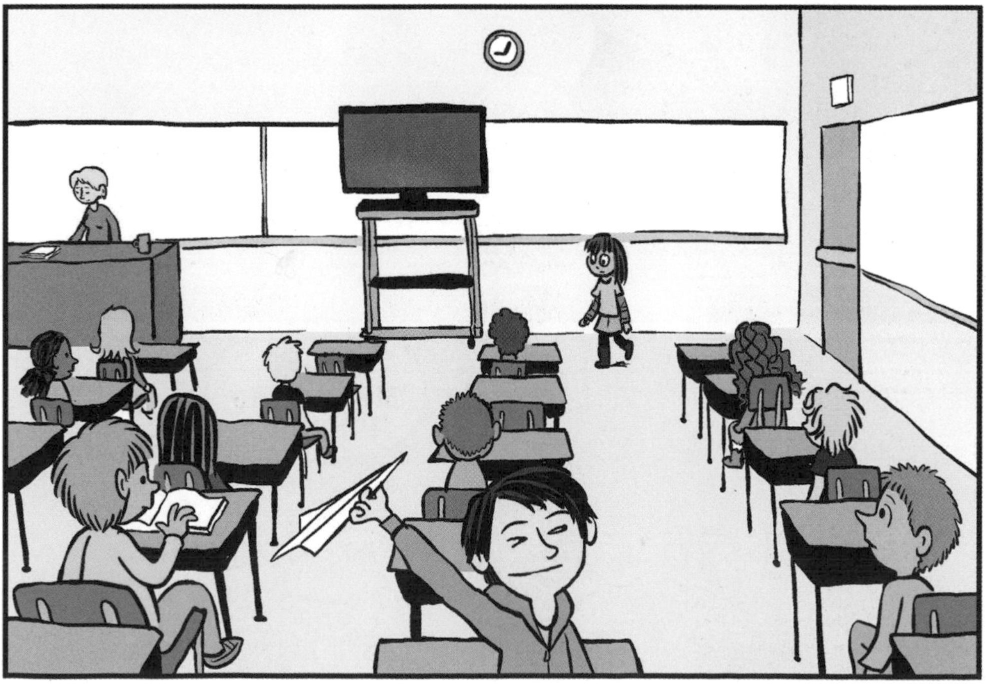

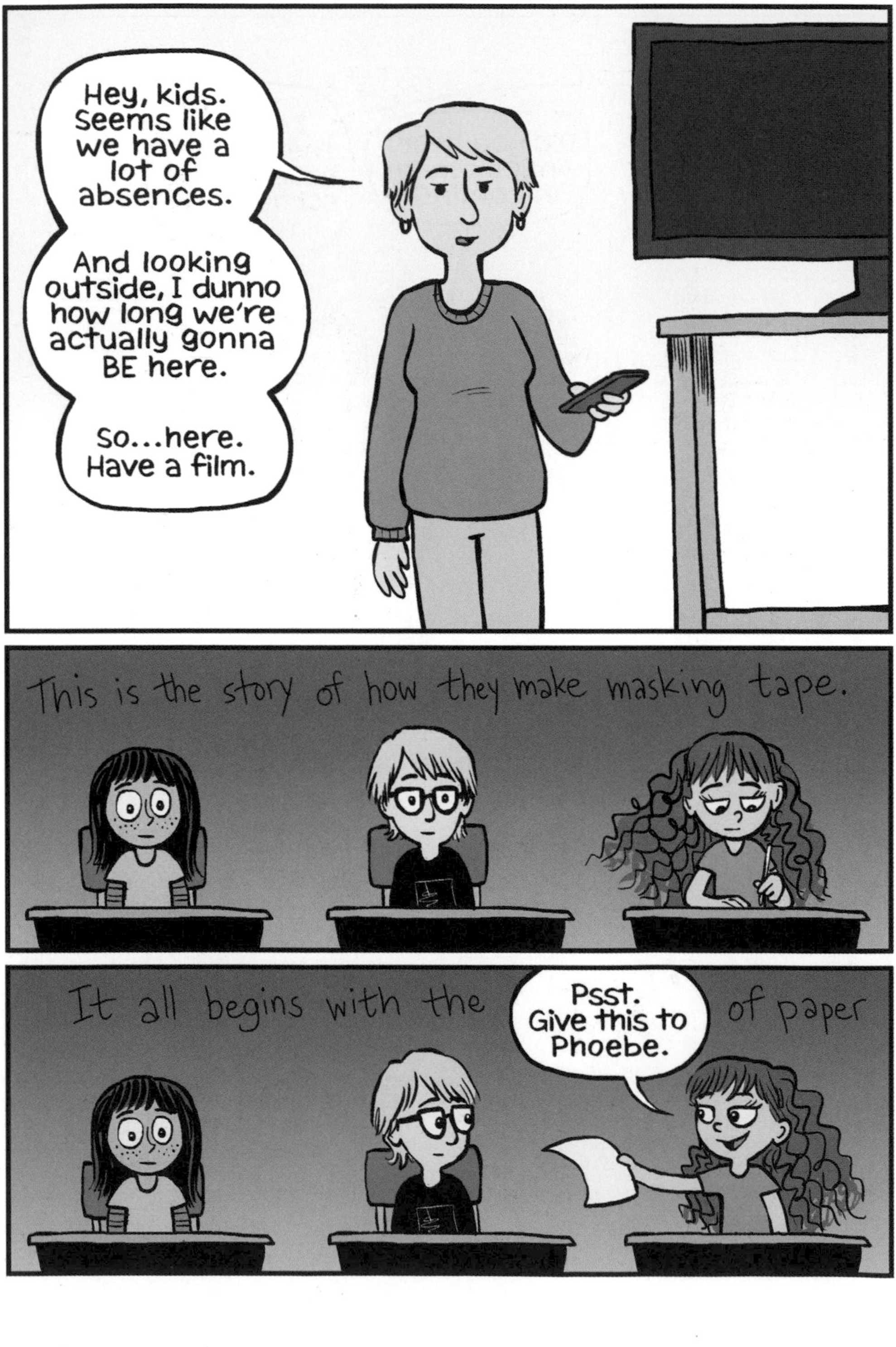
Hey, kids. Seems like we have a lot of absences.
And looking outside, I dunno how long we're actually gonna BE here.
So...here. Have a film.
This is the story of how they make masking tape.
It all begins with the
Psst. Give this to Phoebe.
of paper

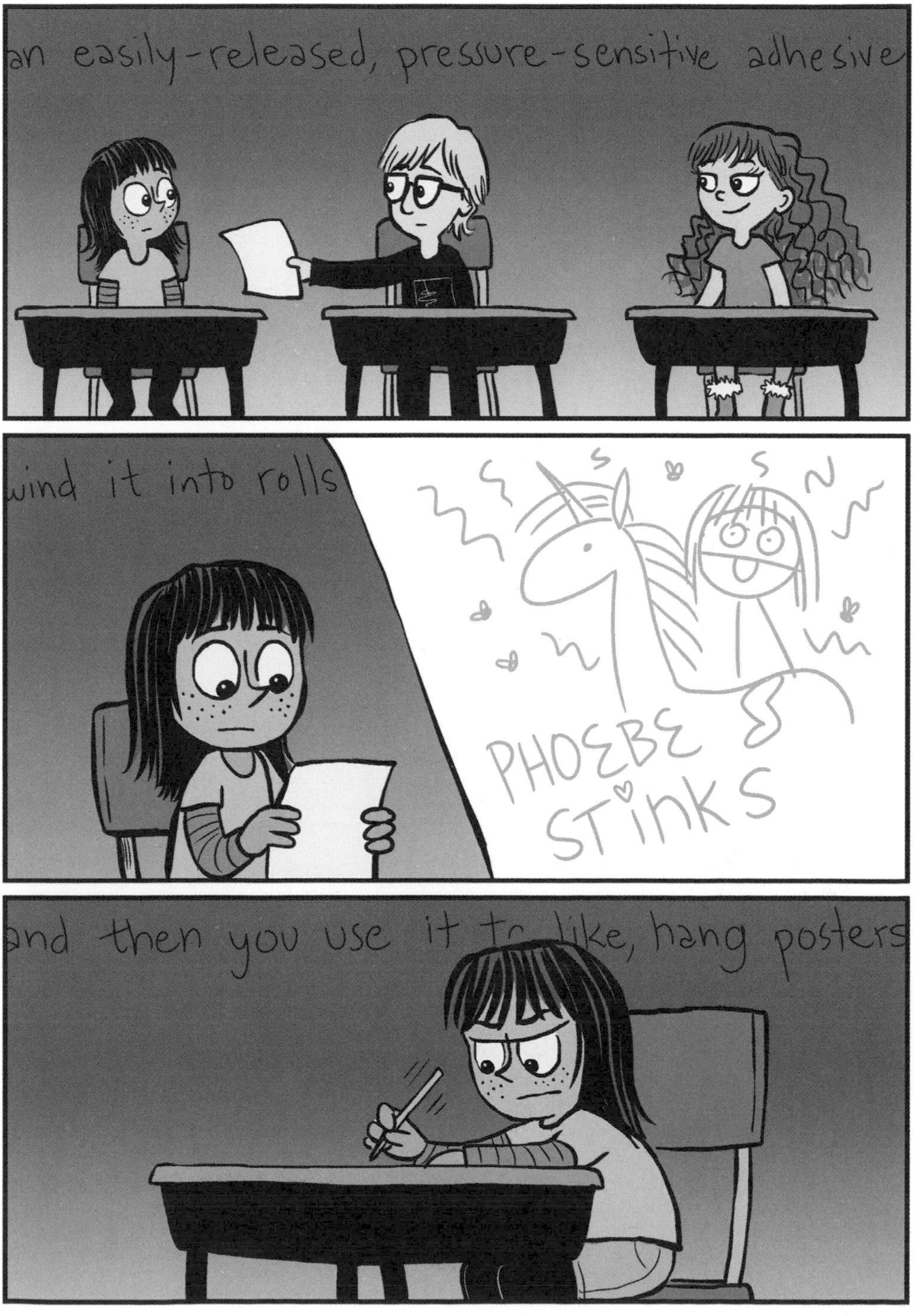
an easily-released, pressure-sensitive adhesive
wind it into rolls
PHOEBE STINKS
and then you use it to like, hang posters

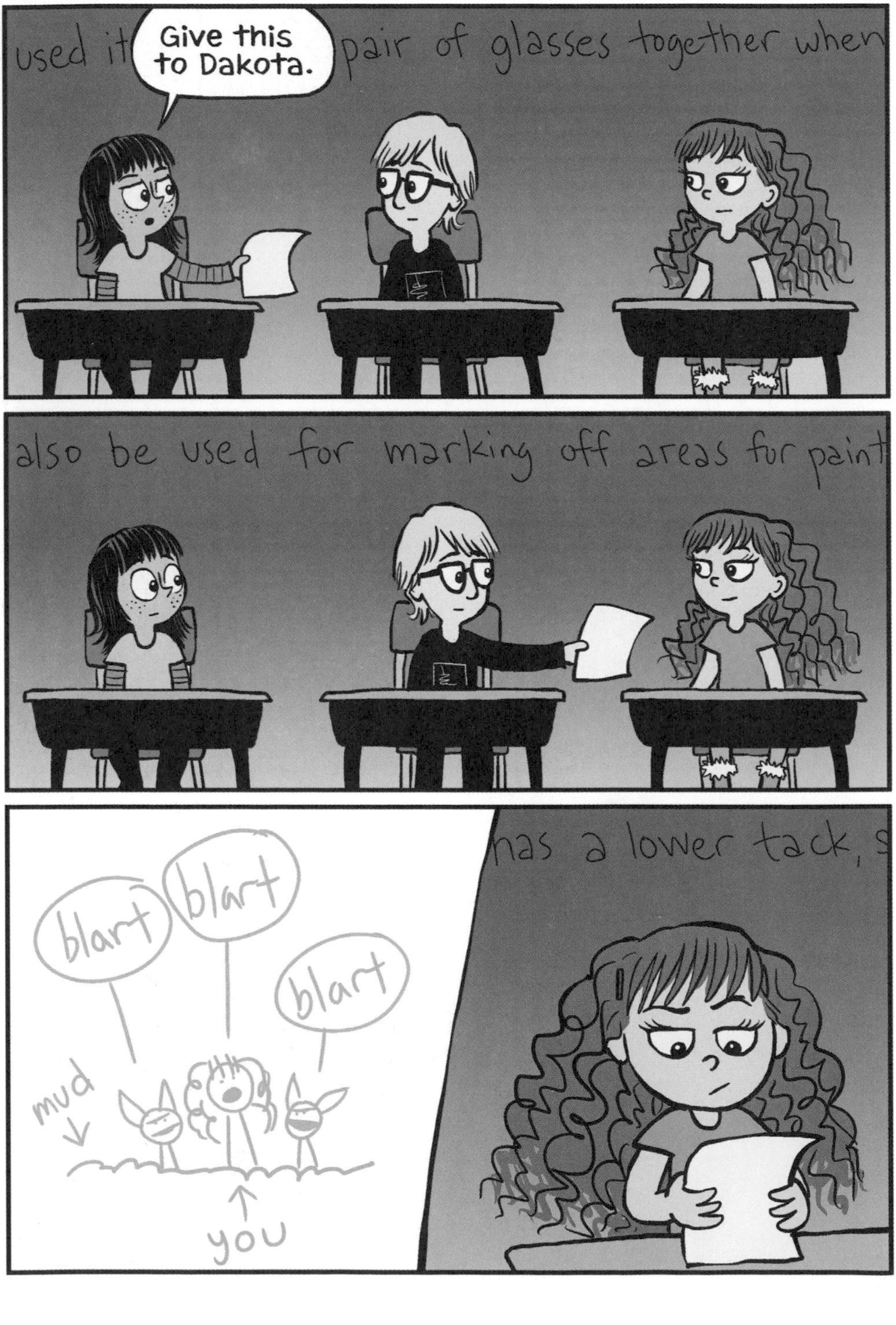
used it
Give this to Dakota.
pair of glasses together when
also be used for marking off areas for paint
blart
blart
blart
mud
you
has a lower tack,

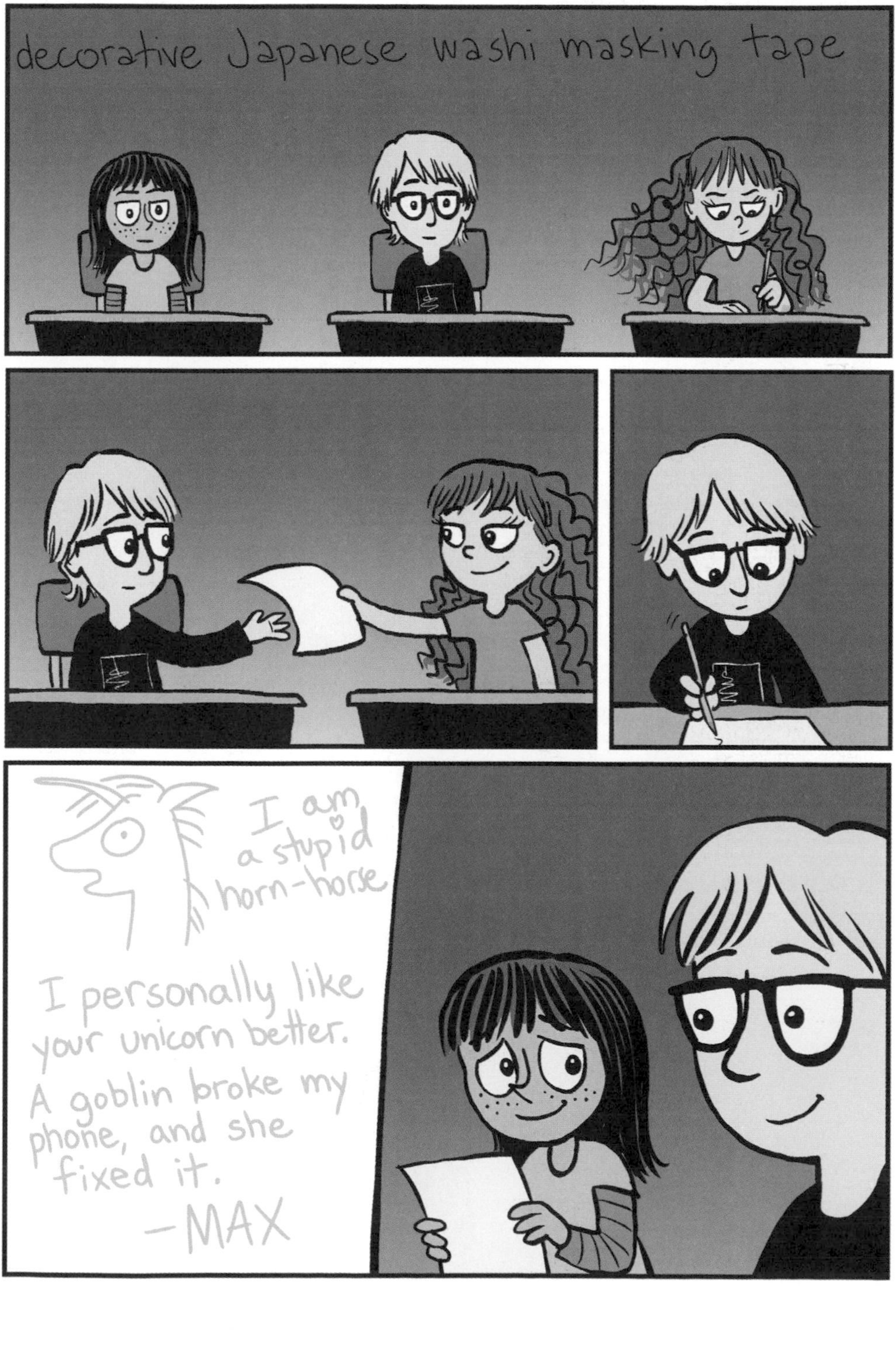
decorative Japanese washi masking tape
I am a stupid horn-horse
I personally like your unicorn better. A goblin broke my phone, and she fixed it.
—MAX

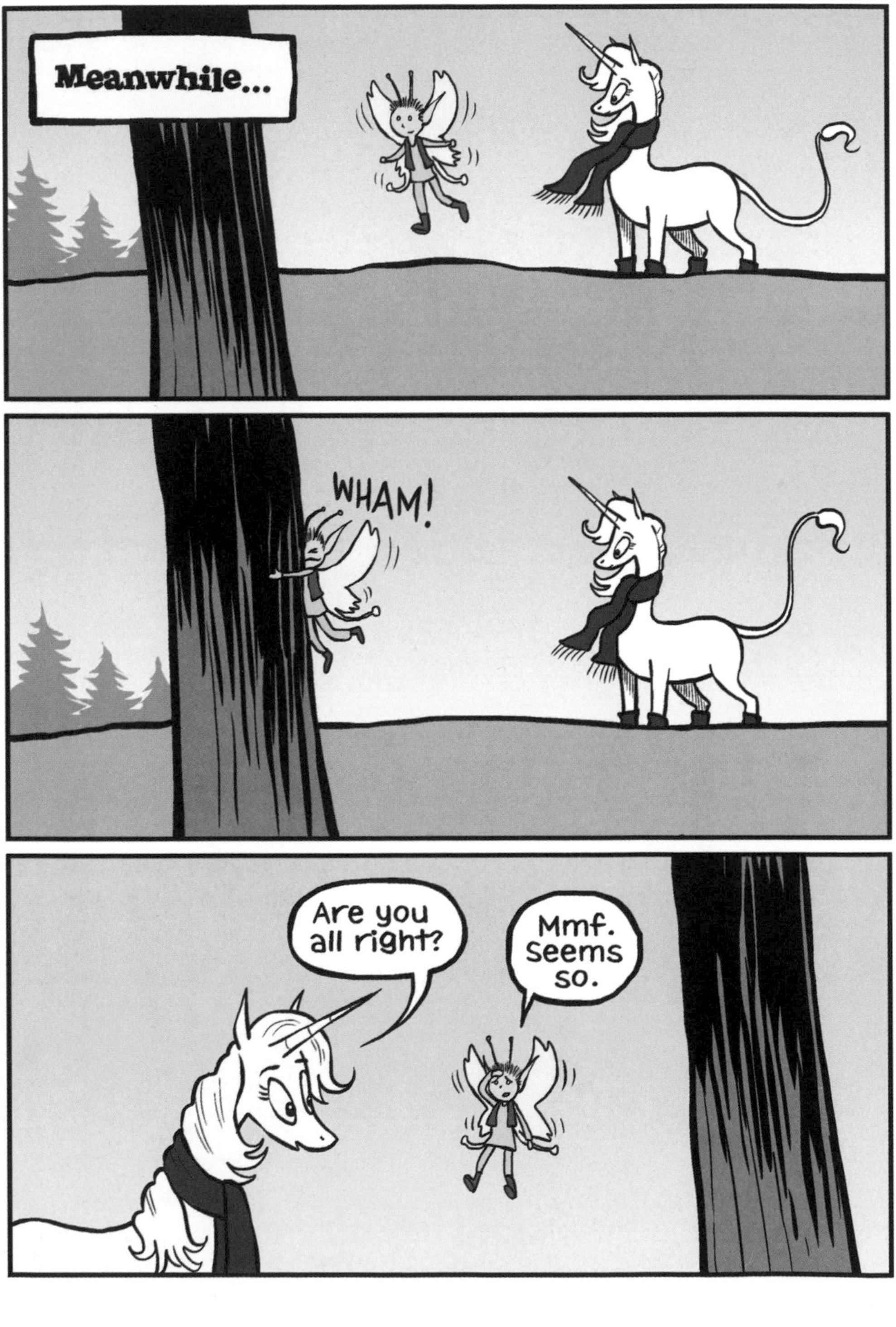
Meanwhile...
WHAM!
Are you all right?
Mmf. Seems so.

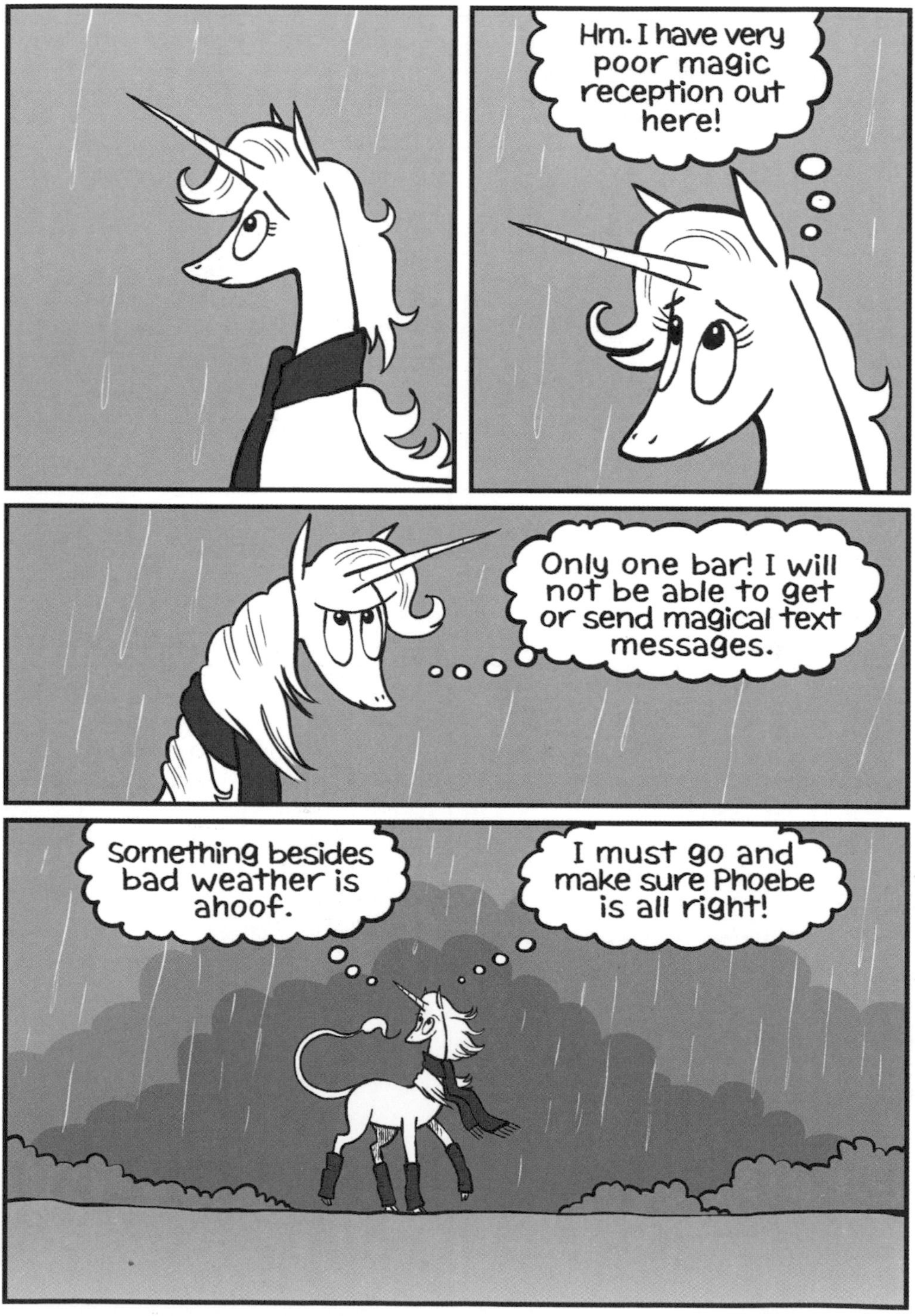
Hm. I have very poor magic reception out here!
Only one bar! I will not be able to get or send magical text messages.
Something besides bad weather is ahoof.
I must go and make sure Phoebe is all right!

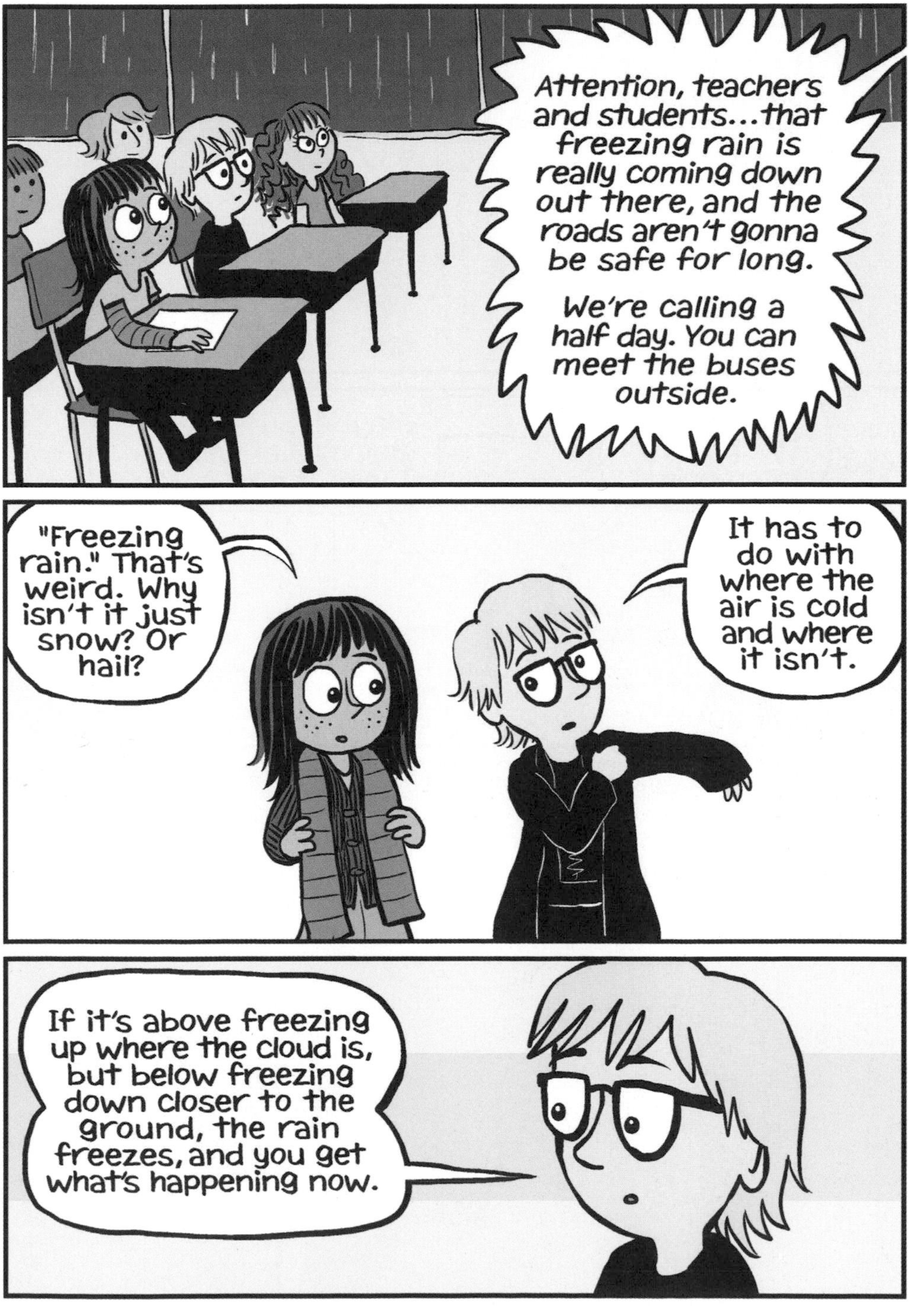
Attention, teachers and students...that freezing rain is really coming down out there, and the roads aren't gonna be safe for long.
We're calling a half day. You can meet the buses outside.
"Freezing rain." That's weird. Why isn't it just snow? Or hail?
It has to do with where the air is cold and where it isn't.
If it's above freezing up where the cloud is, but below freezing down closer to the ground, the rain freezes, and you get what's happening now.

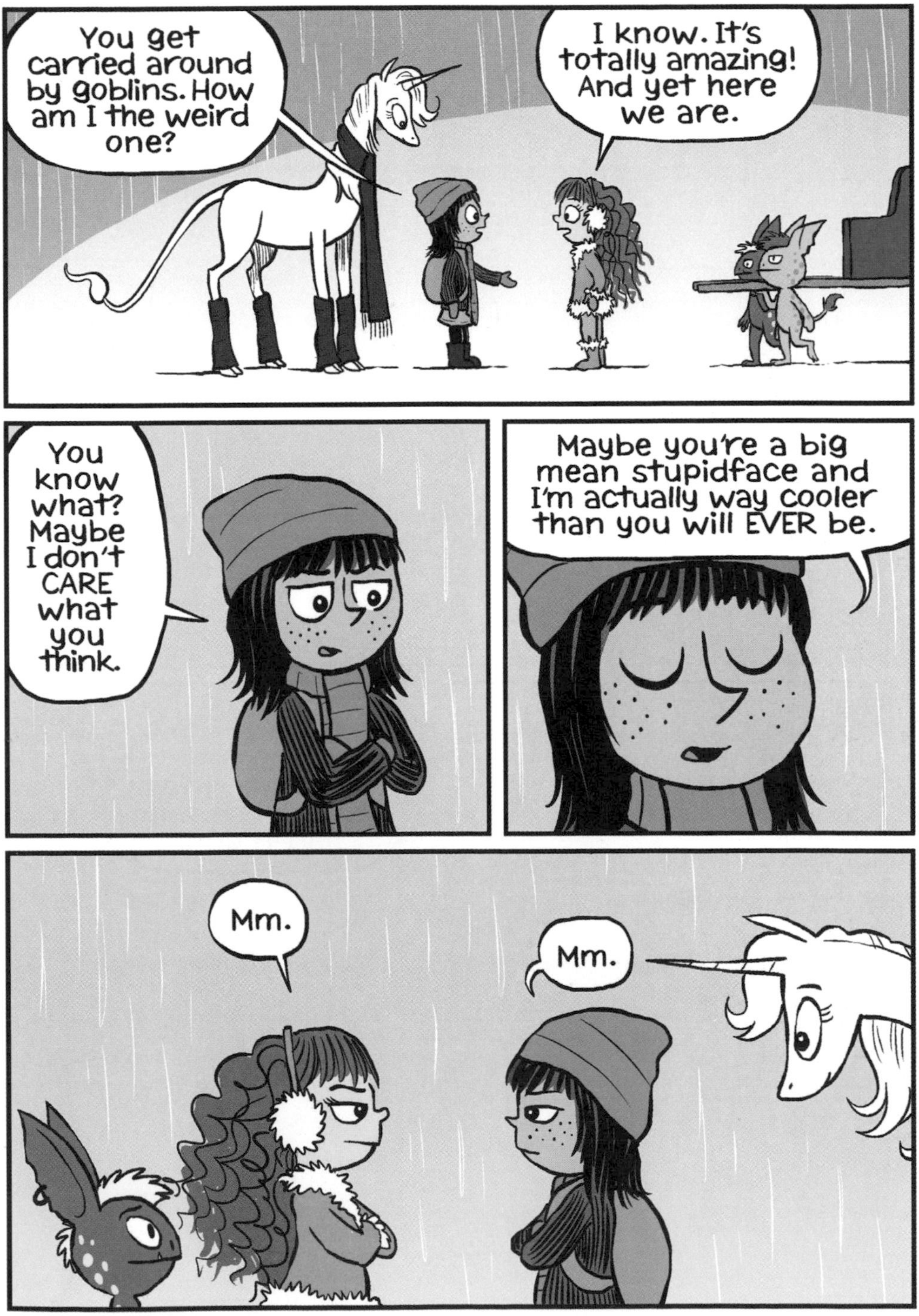
You get carried around by goblins. How am I the weird one?
I know. It's totally amazing! And yet here we are.
You know what? Maybe I don't CARE what you think.
Maybe you're a big mean stupidface and I'm actually way cooler than you will EVER be.
Mm.
Mm.

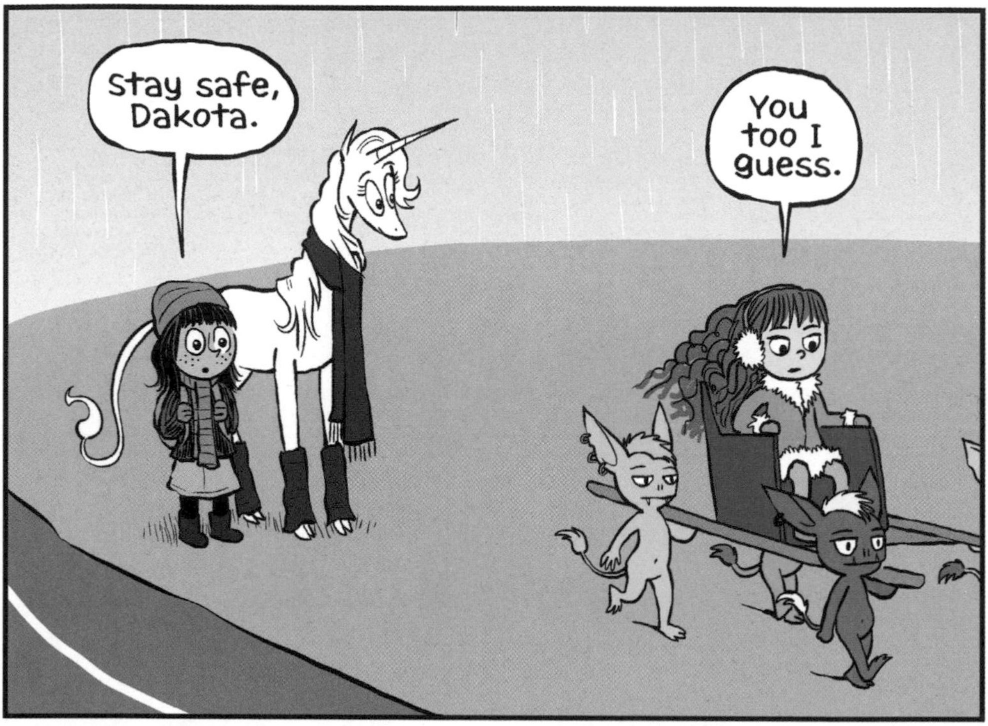
Stay safe, Dakota.
You too I guess.

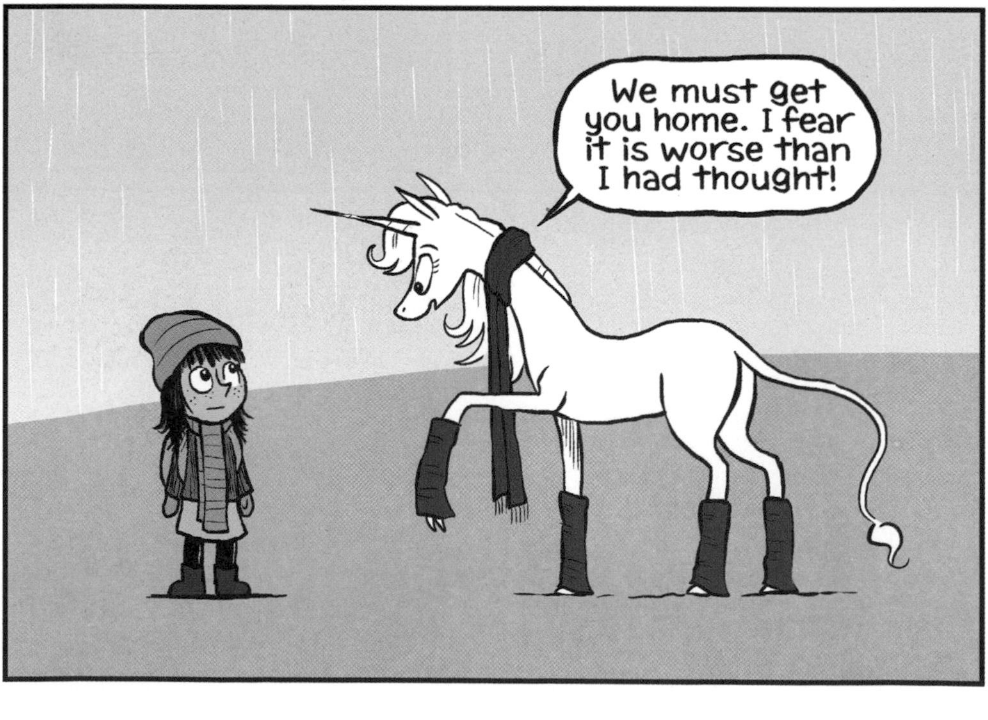
We must get you home. I fear it is worse than I had thought!

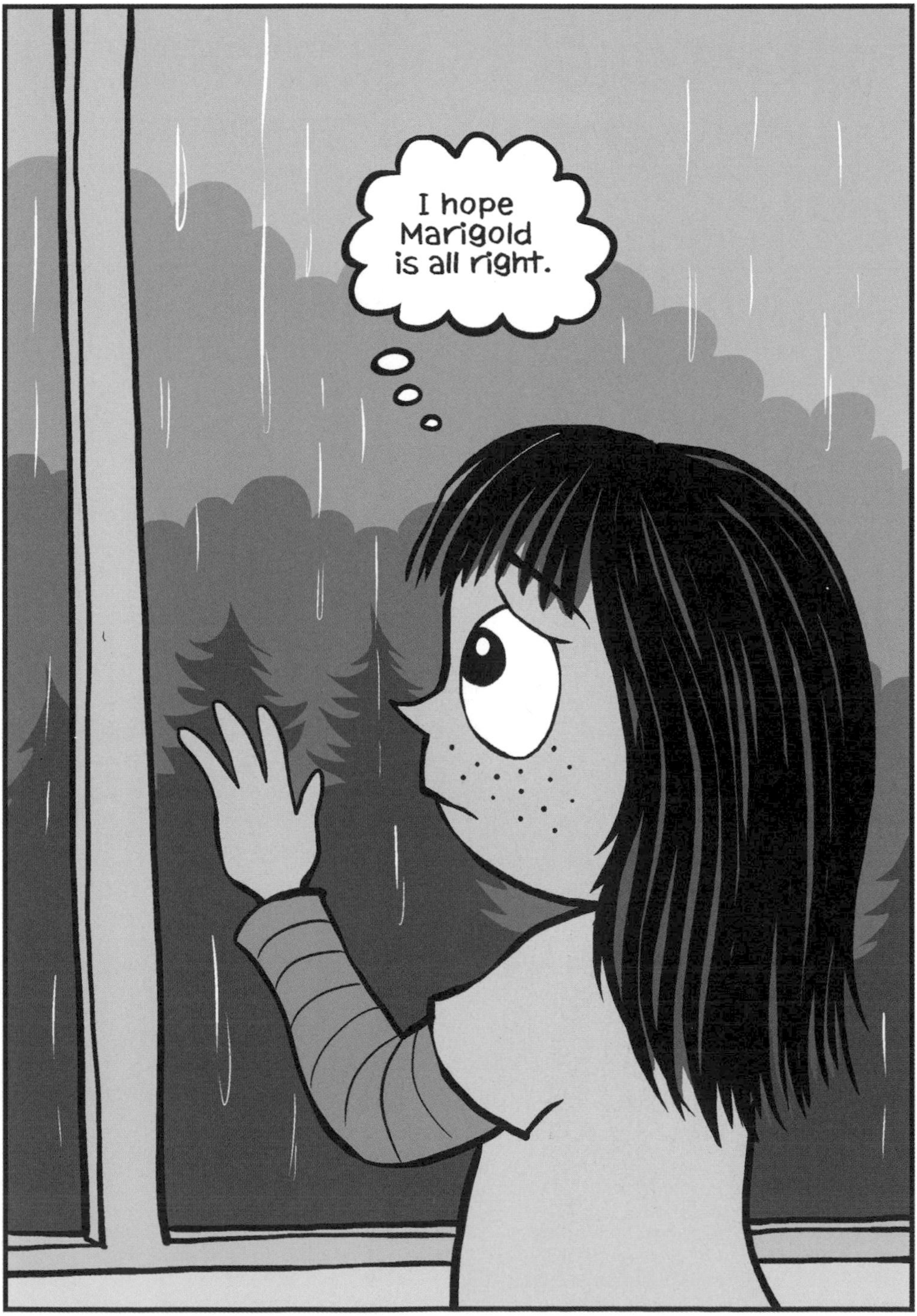
I hope Marigold is all right.

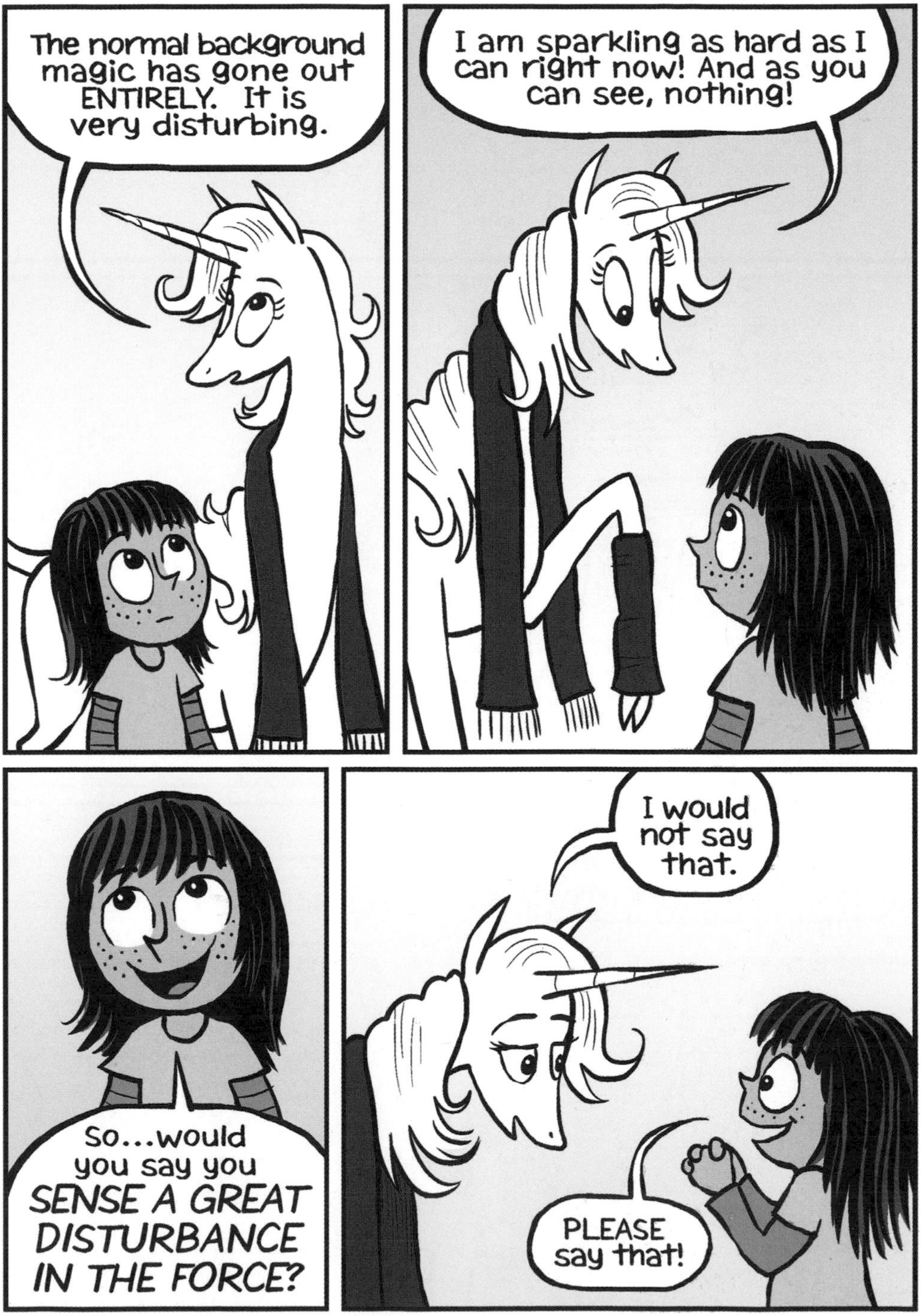
The normal background magic has gone out ENTIRELY. It is very disturbing.
I am sparkling as hard as I can right now! And as you can see, nothing!
So...would you say you SENSE A GREAT DISTURBANCE IN THE FORCE?
I would not say that.
PLEASE say that!

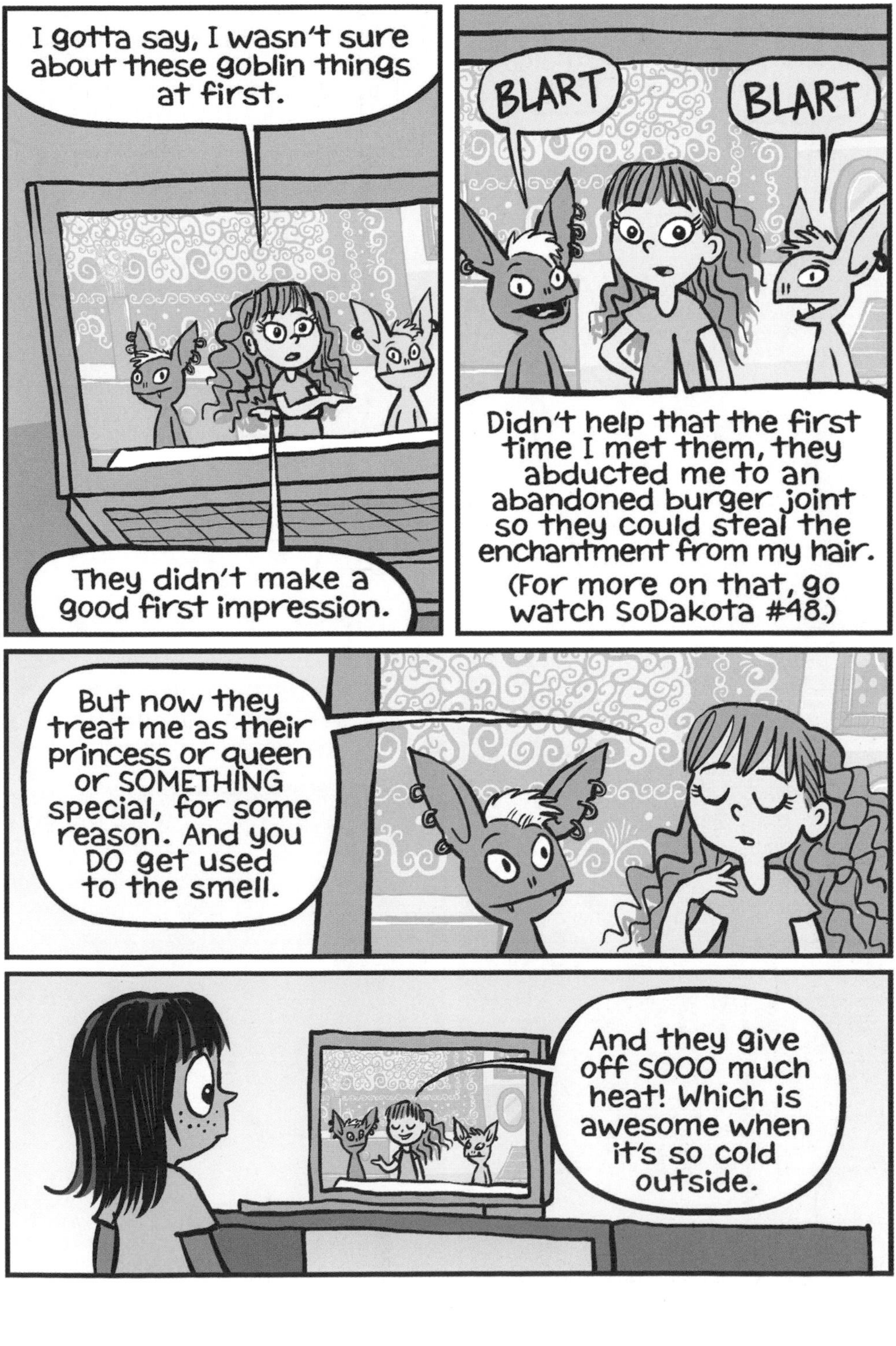
I gotta say, I wasn't sure about these goblin things at first.
They didn't make a good first impression.
BLART
BLART
Didn't help that the first time I met them, they abducted me to an abandoned burger joint so they could steal the enchantment from my hair.
(For more on that, go watch SoDakota #48.)
But now they treat me as their princess or queen or SOMETHING special, for some reason. And you DO get used to the smell.
And they give off SOOO much heat! Which is awesome when it's so cold outside.

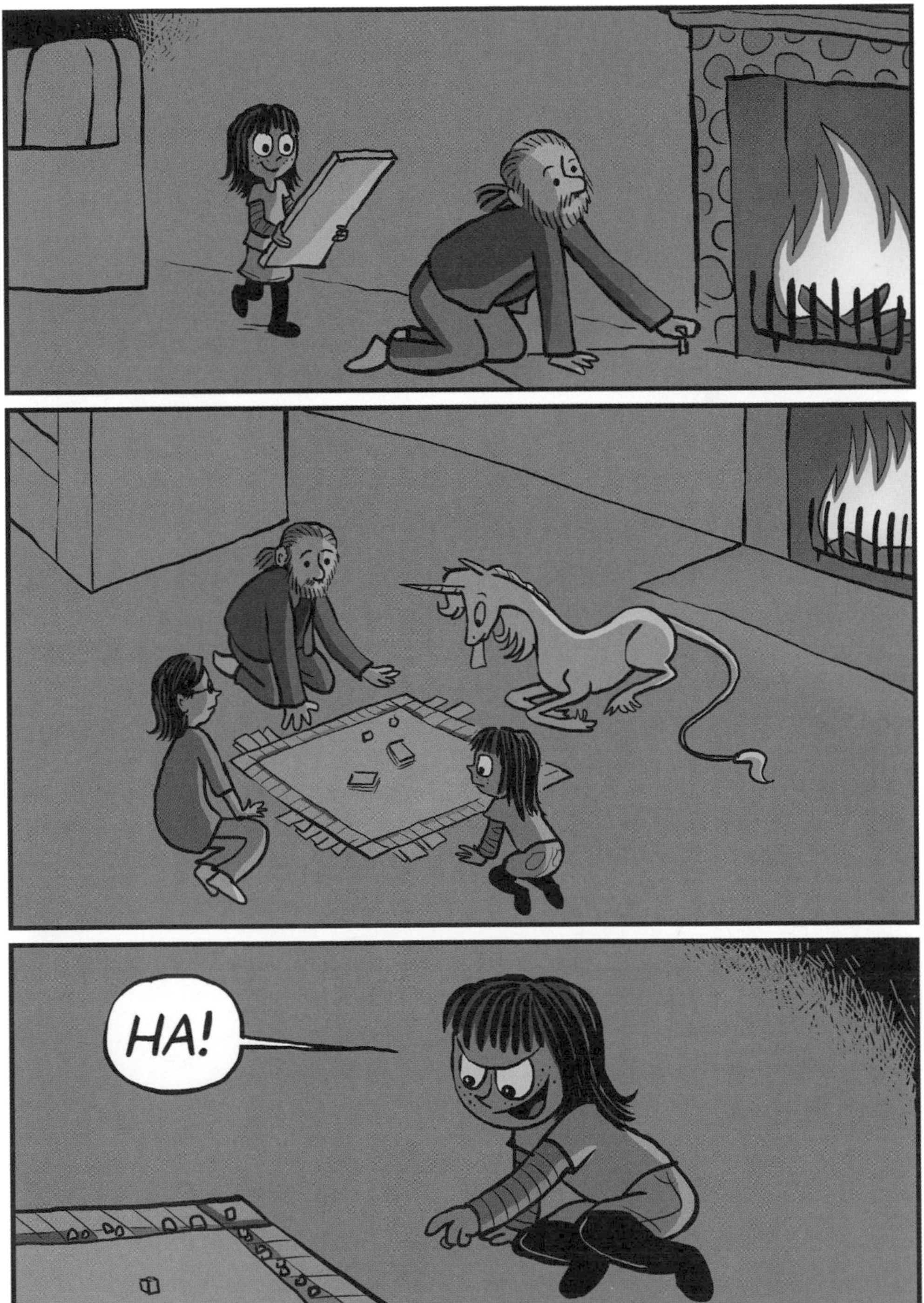
HA!

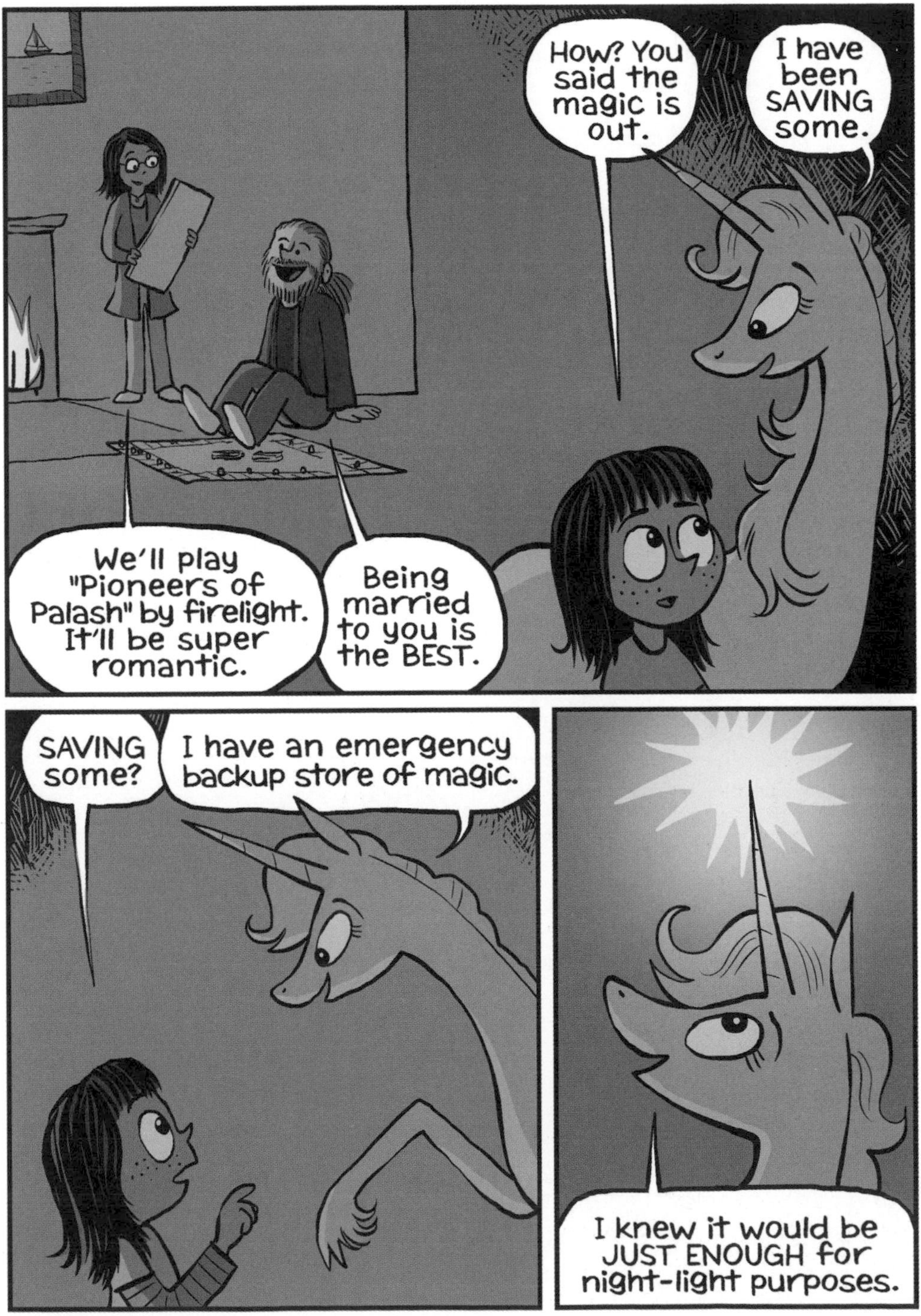
How? You said the magic is out.
I have been SAVING some.
We'll play "Pioneers of Palash" by firelight. It'll be super romantic.
Being married to you is the BEST.
SAVING some?
I have an emergency backup store of magic.
I knew it would be JUST ENOUGH for night-light purposes.

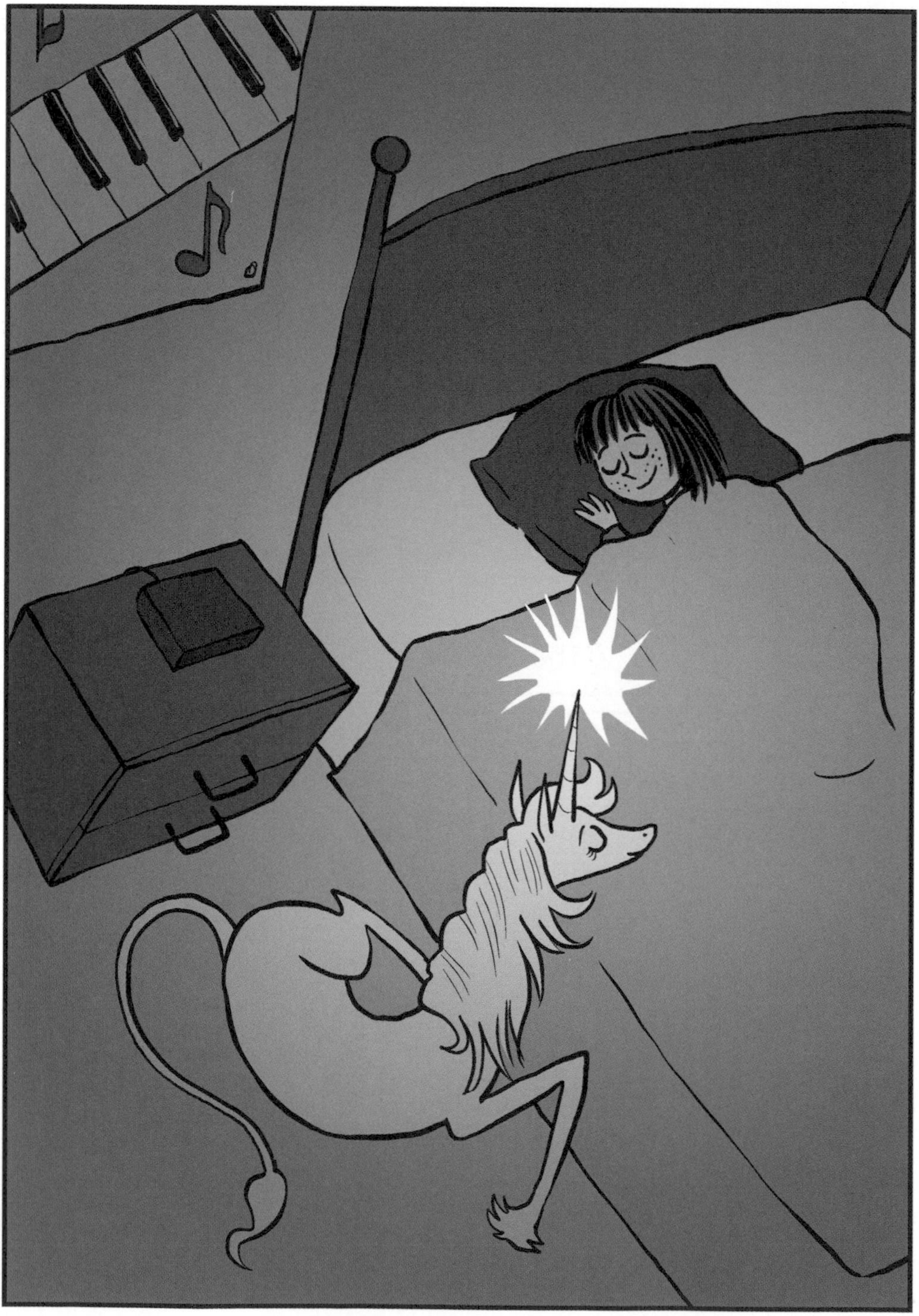

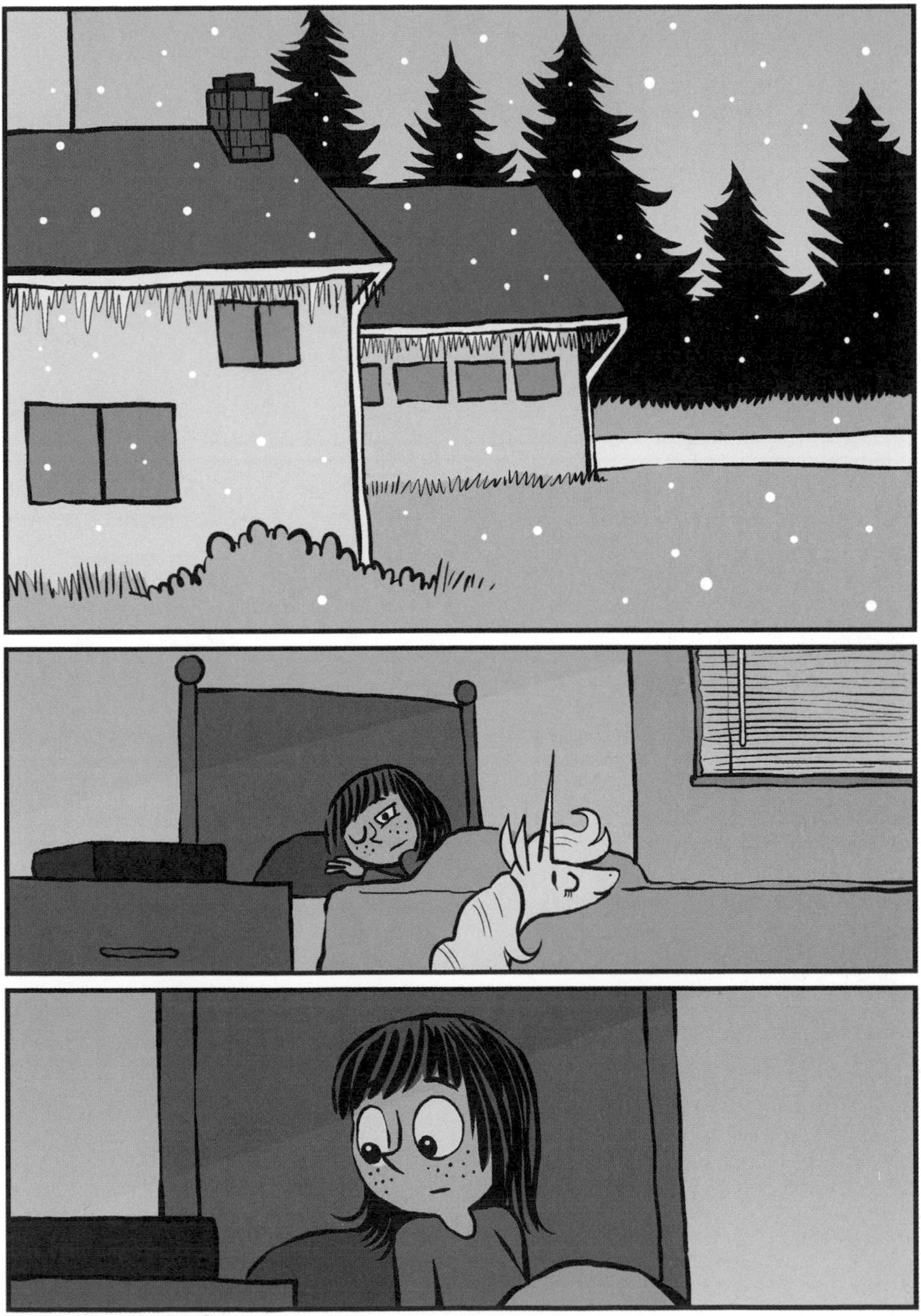

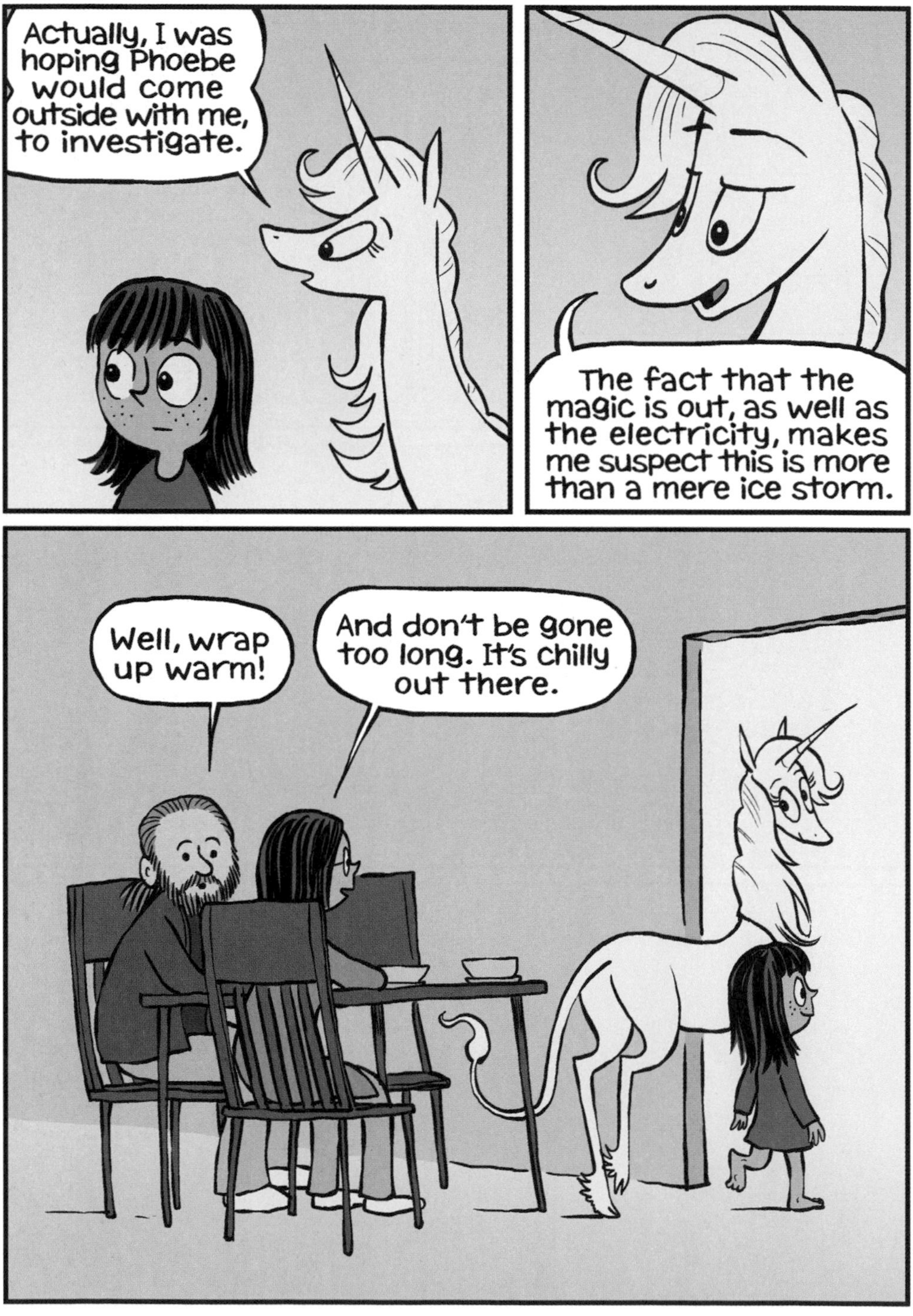

Actually, I was hoping Phoebe would come outside with me, to investigate.
The fact that the magic is out, as well as the electricity, makes me suspect this is more than a mere ice storm.
Well, wrap up warm!
And don't be gone too long. It's chilly out there.

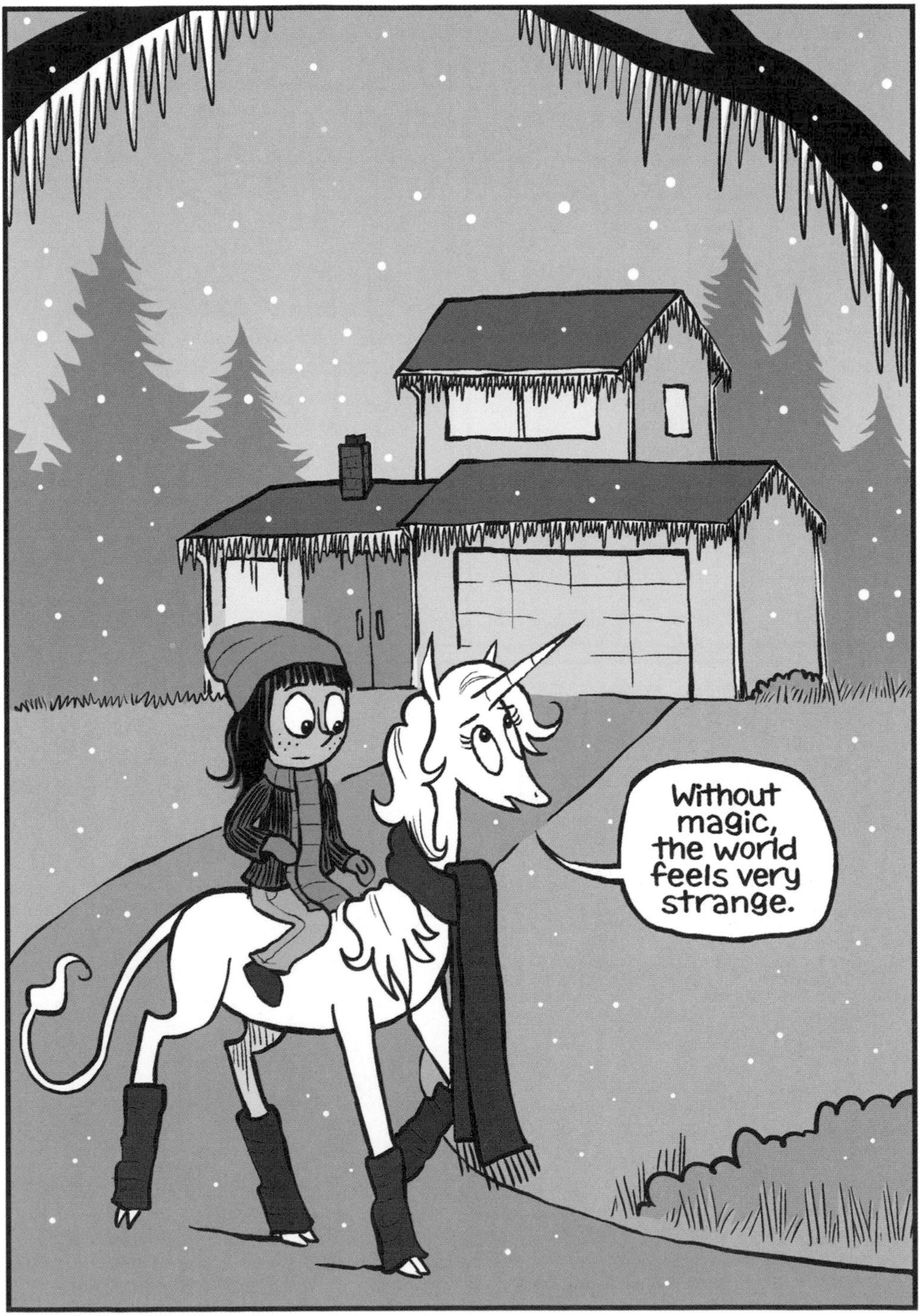
Without magic, the world feels very strange.

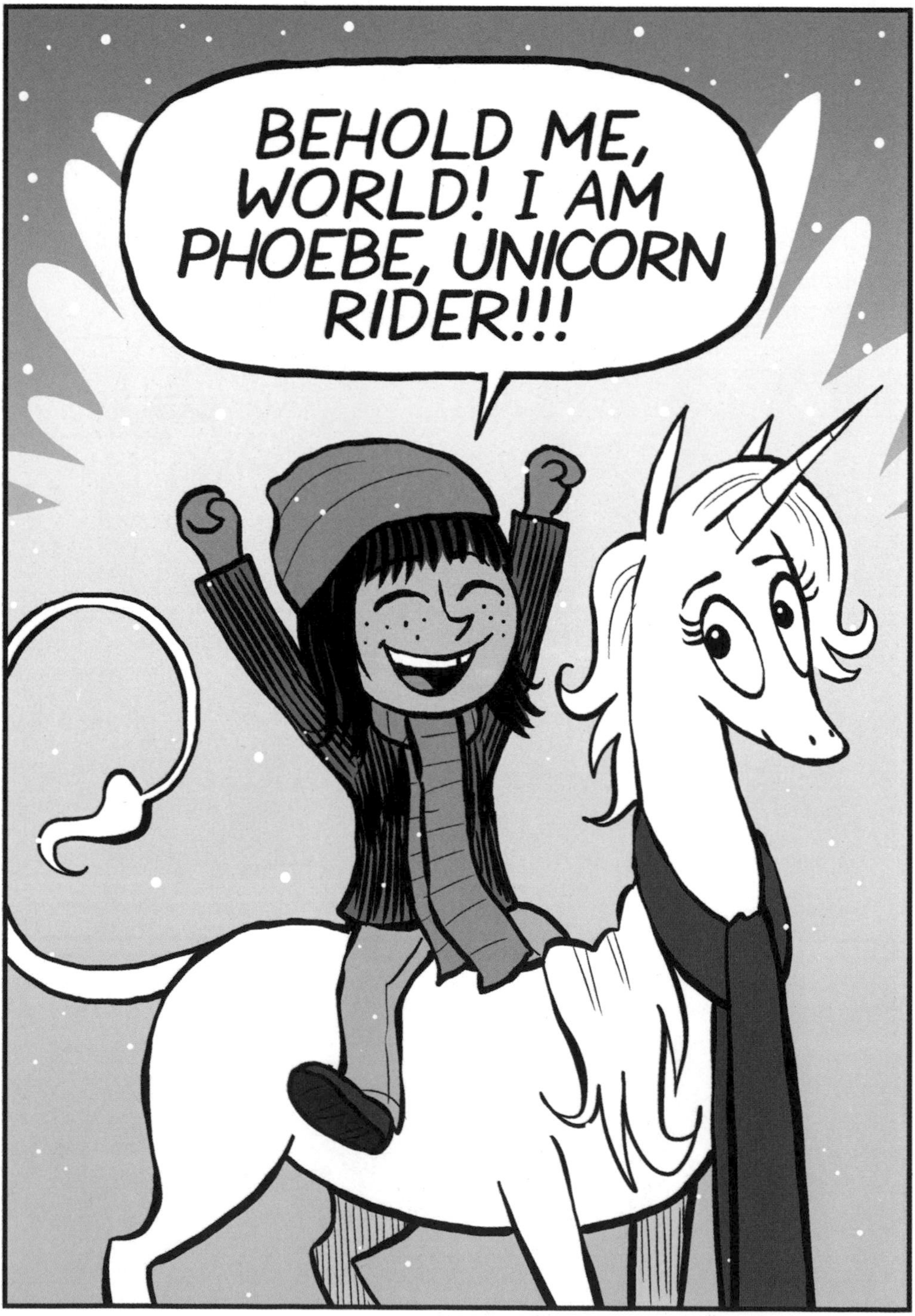
BEHOLD ME, WORLD! I AM PHOEBE, UNICORN RIDER!!!

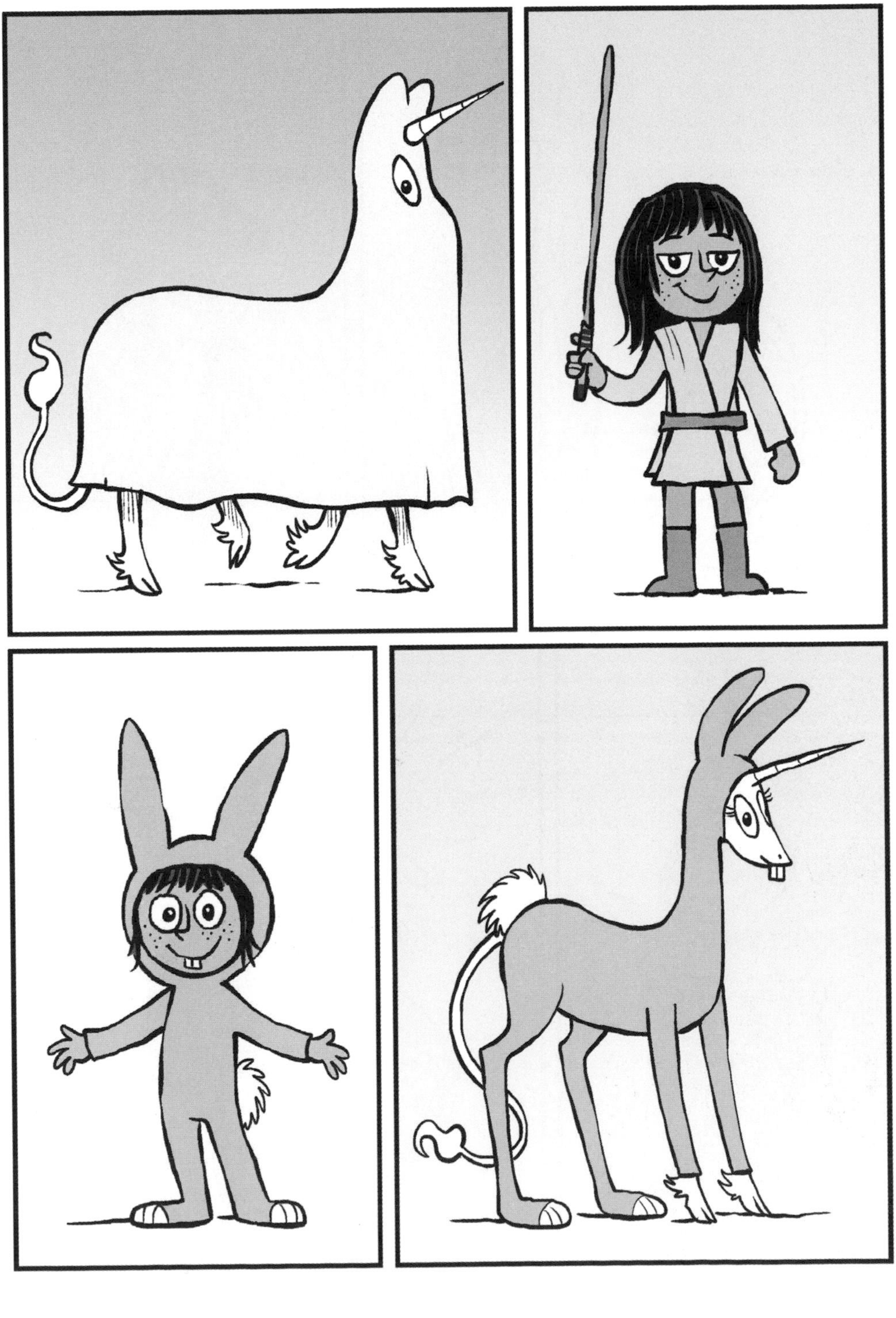

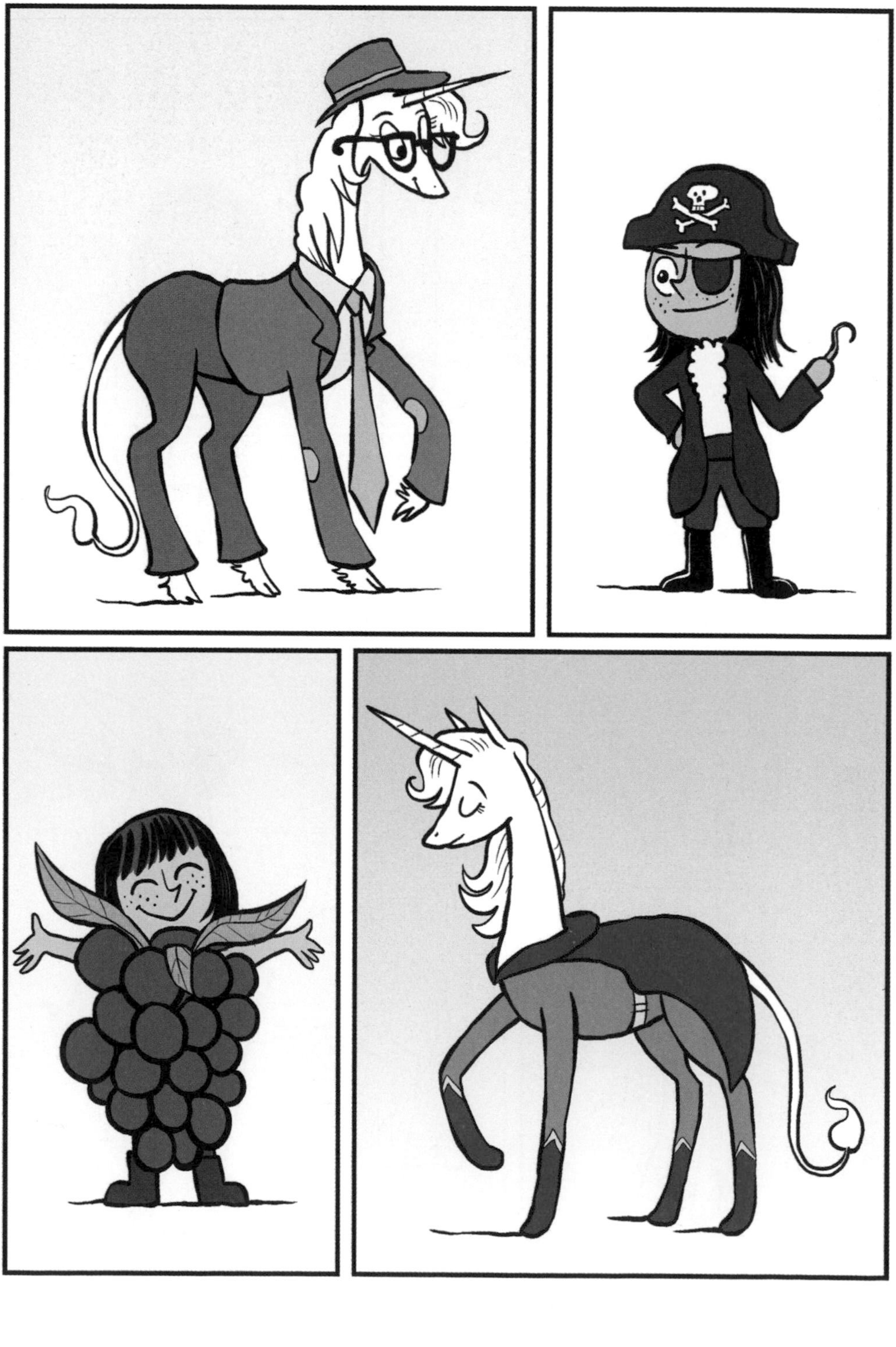

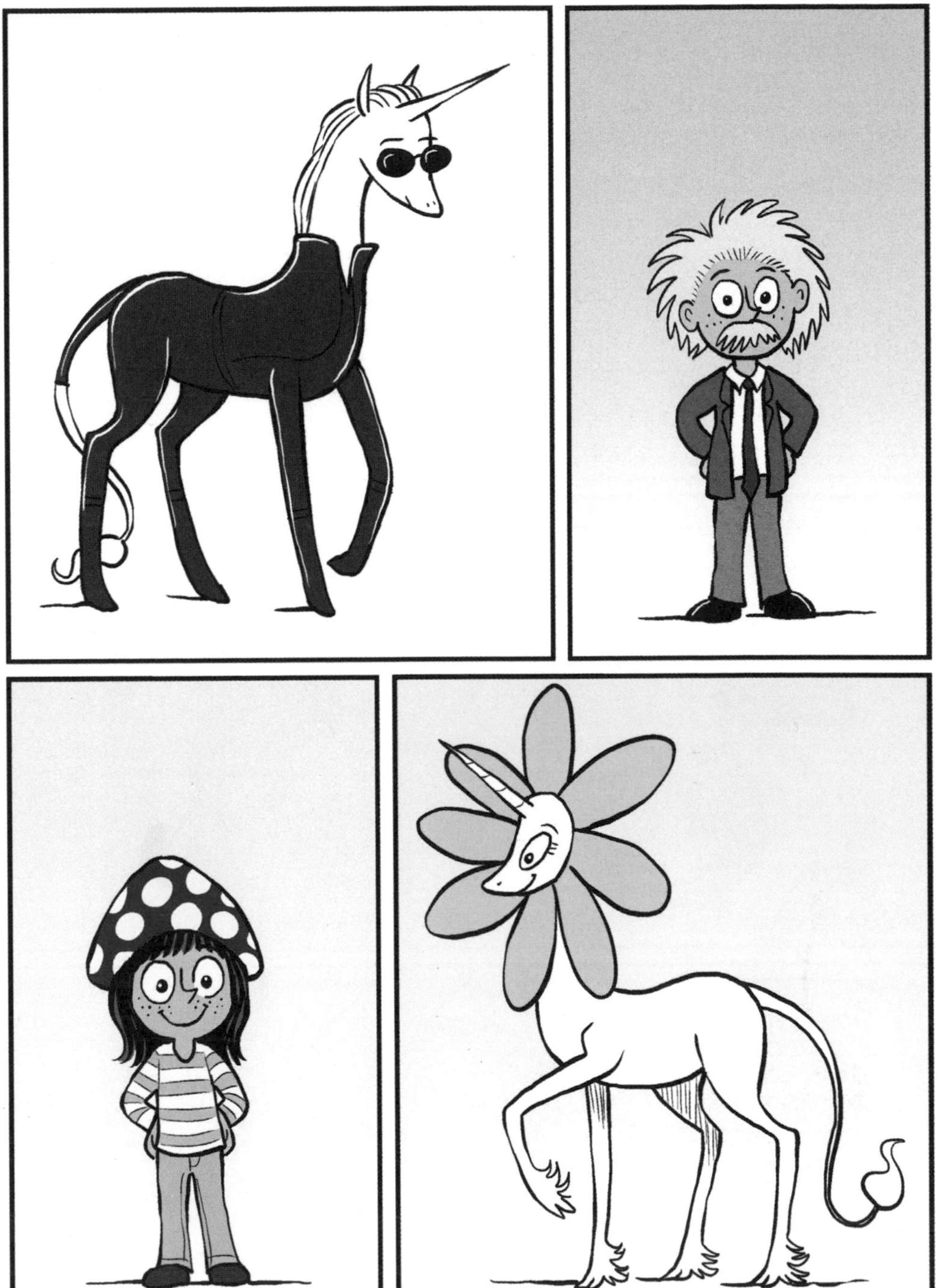

62

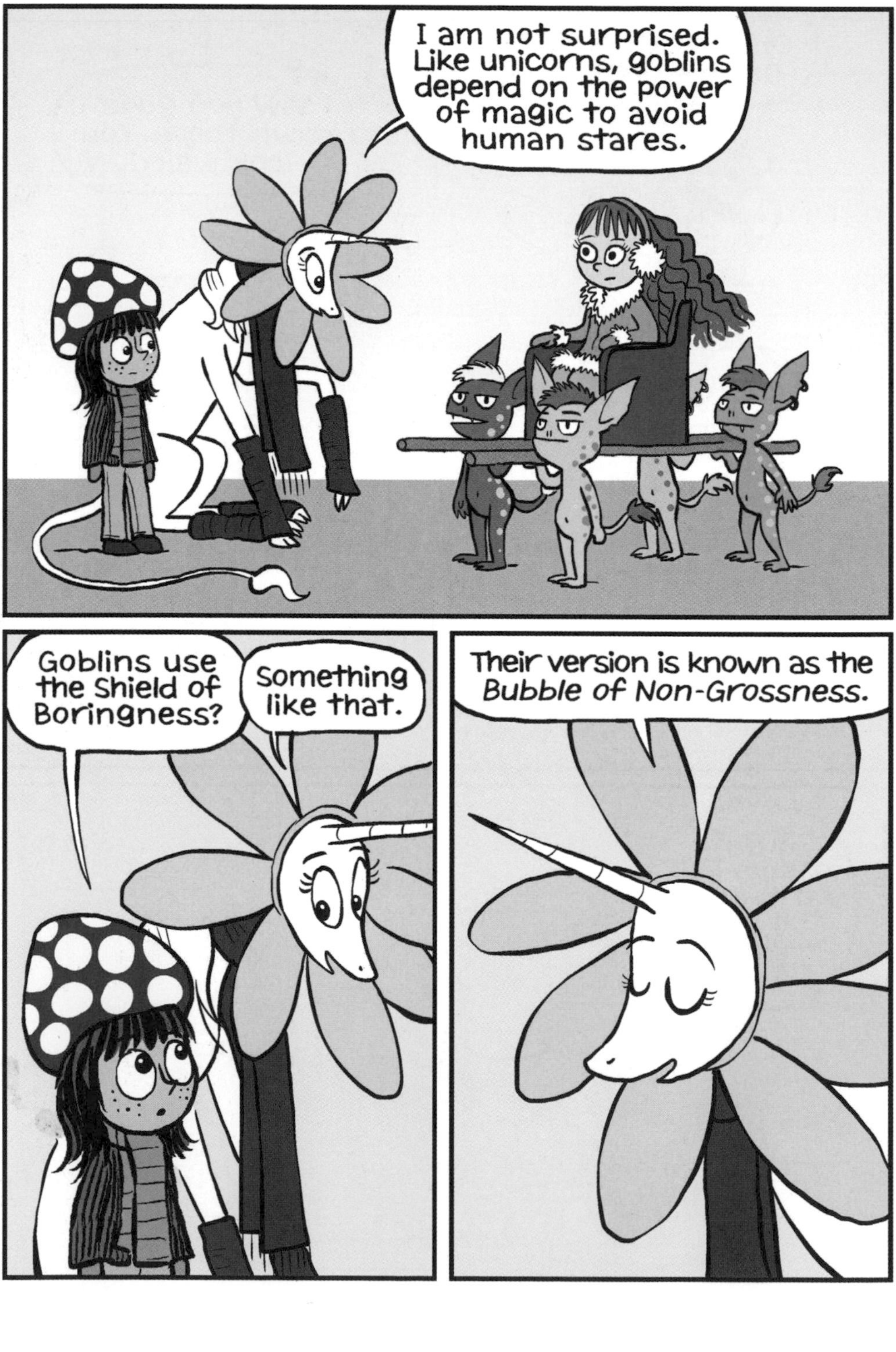
I am not surprised. Like unicorns, goblins depend on the power of magic to avoid human stares.
Goblins use the Shield of Boringness?
Something like that.
Their version is known as the *Bubble of Non-Grossness.*

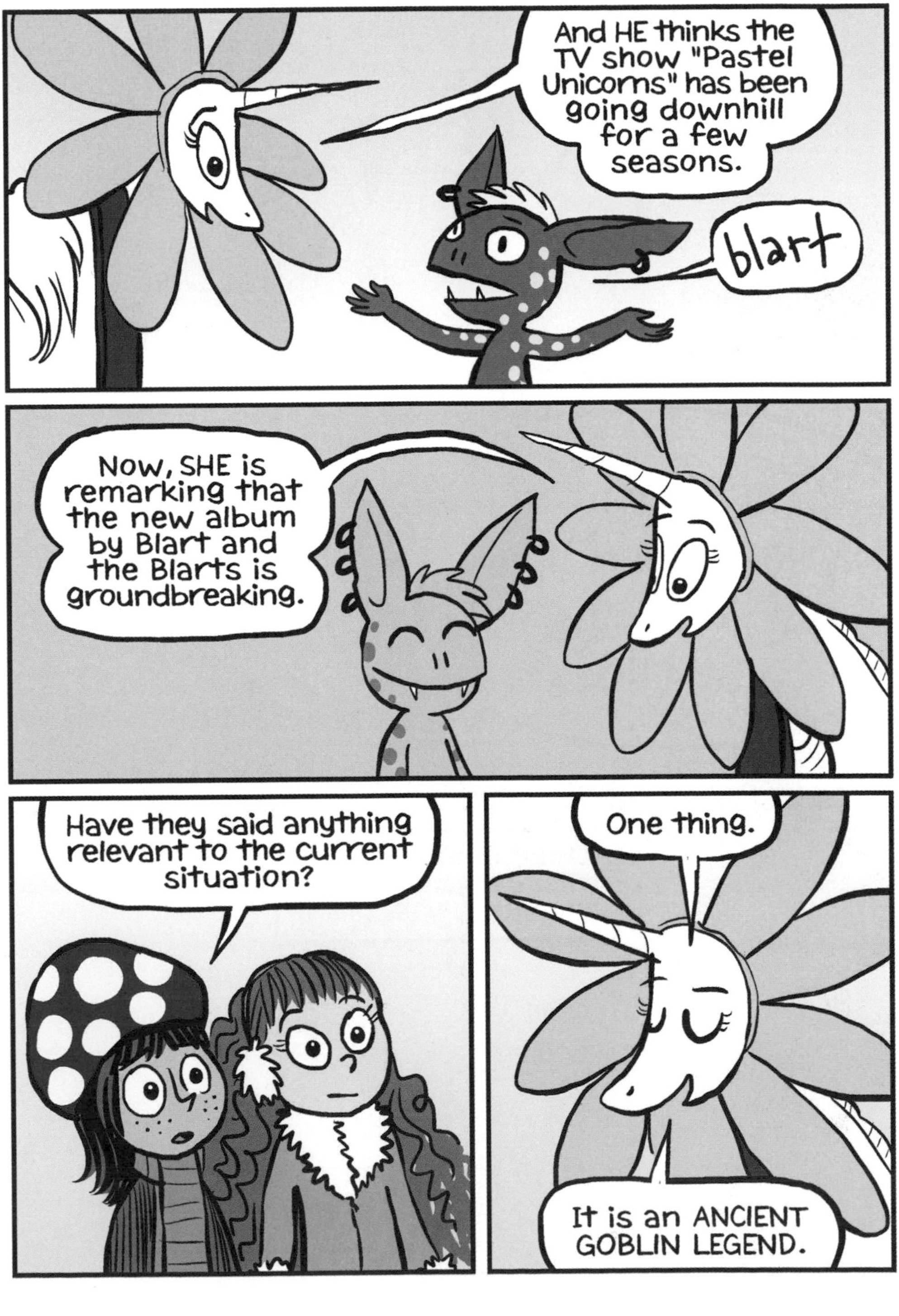
And HE thinks the TV show "Pastel Unicorns" has been going downhill for a few seasons.
blart
Now, SHE is remarking that the new album by Blart and the Blarts is groundbreaking.
Have they said anything relevant to the current situation?
One thing.
It is an ANCIENT GOBLIN LEGEND.

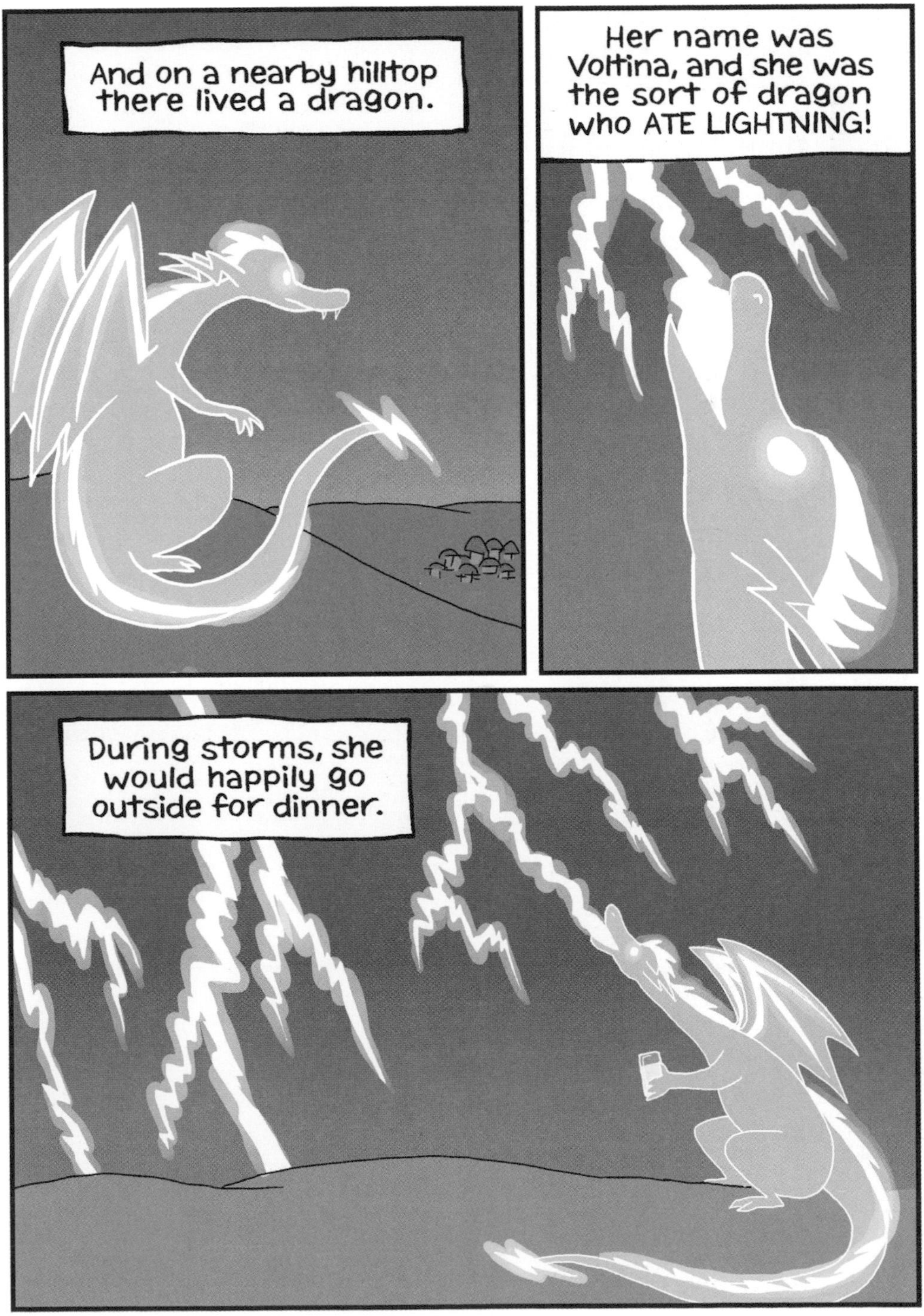
And on a nearby hilltop there lived a dragon.
Her name was Voltina, and she was the sort of dragon who ATE LIGHTNING!
During storms, she would happily go outside for dinner.

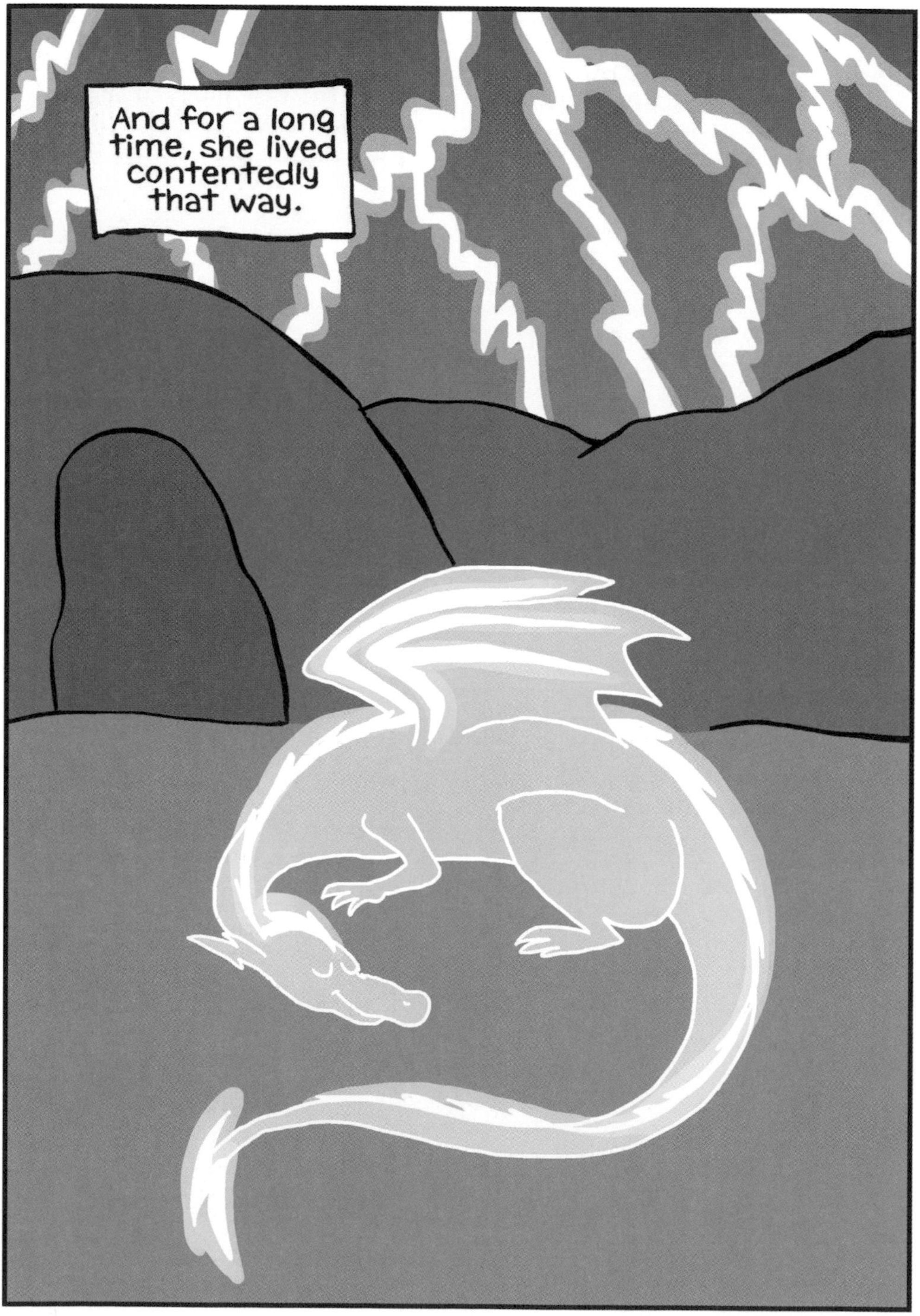
And for a long time, she lived contentedly that way.

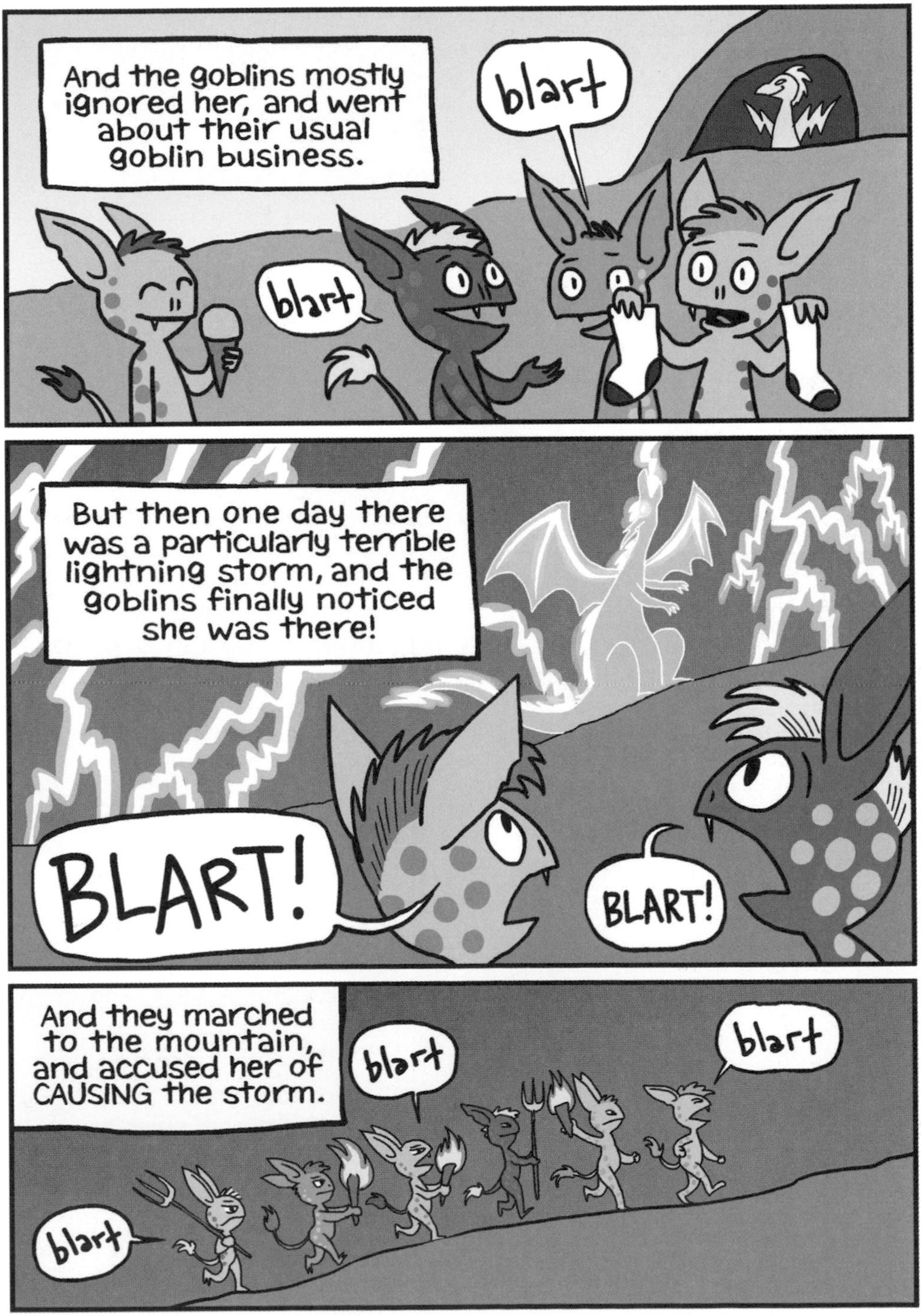
And the goblins mostly ignored her, and went about their usual goblin business.
blart
blart
But then one day there was a particularly terrible lightning storm, and the goblins finally noticed she was there!
BLART!
BLART!
And they marched to the mountain, and accused her of CAUSING the storm.
blart
blart
blart

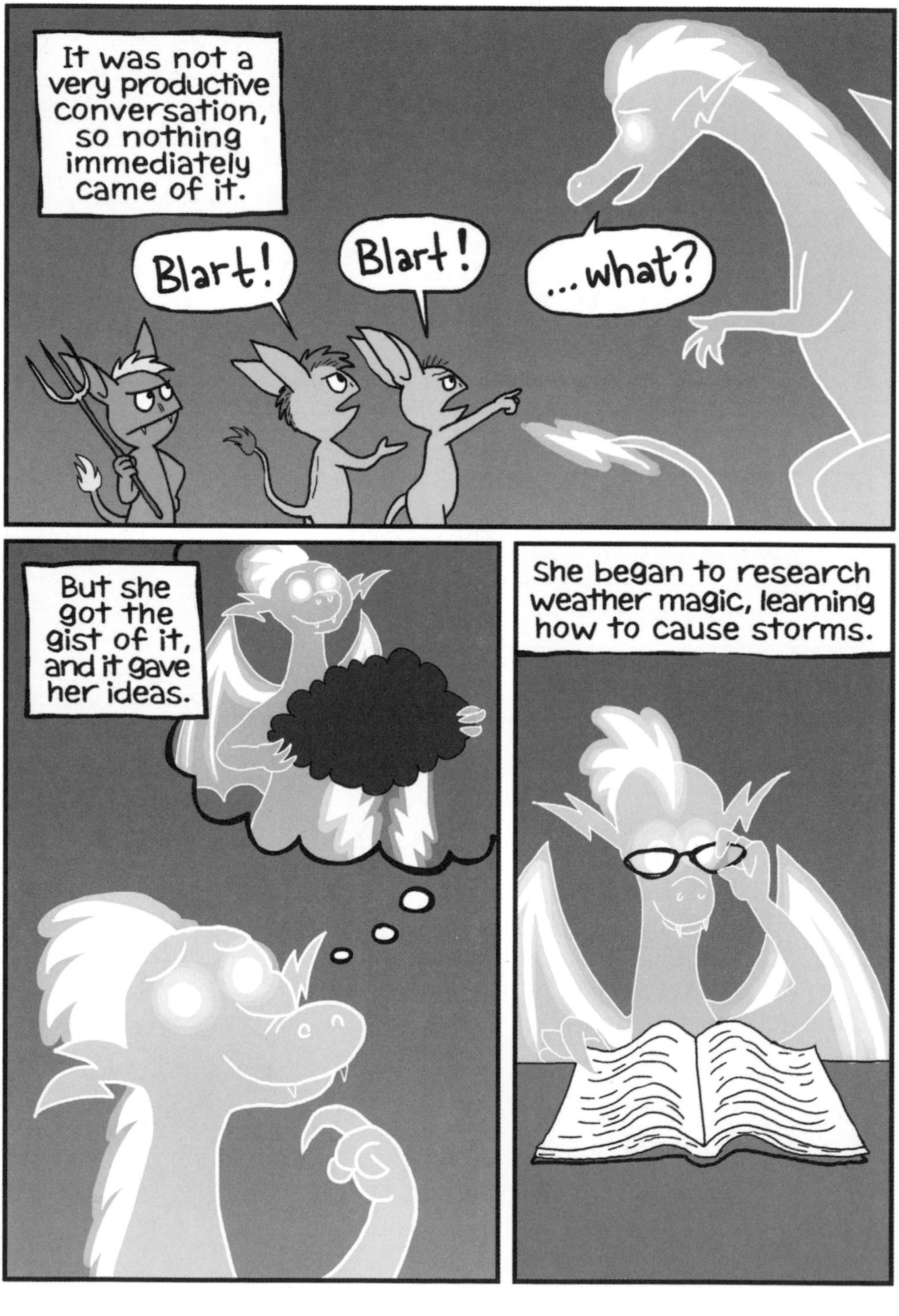

It was not a very productive conversation, so nothing immediately came of it.
Blart!
Blart!
...what?
But she got the gist of it, and it gave her ideas.
She began to research weather magic, learning how to cause storms.

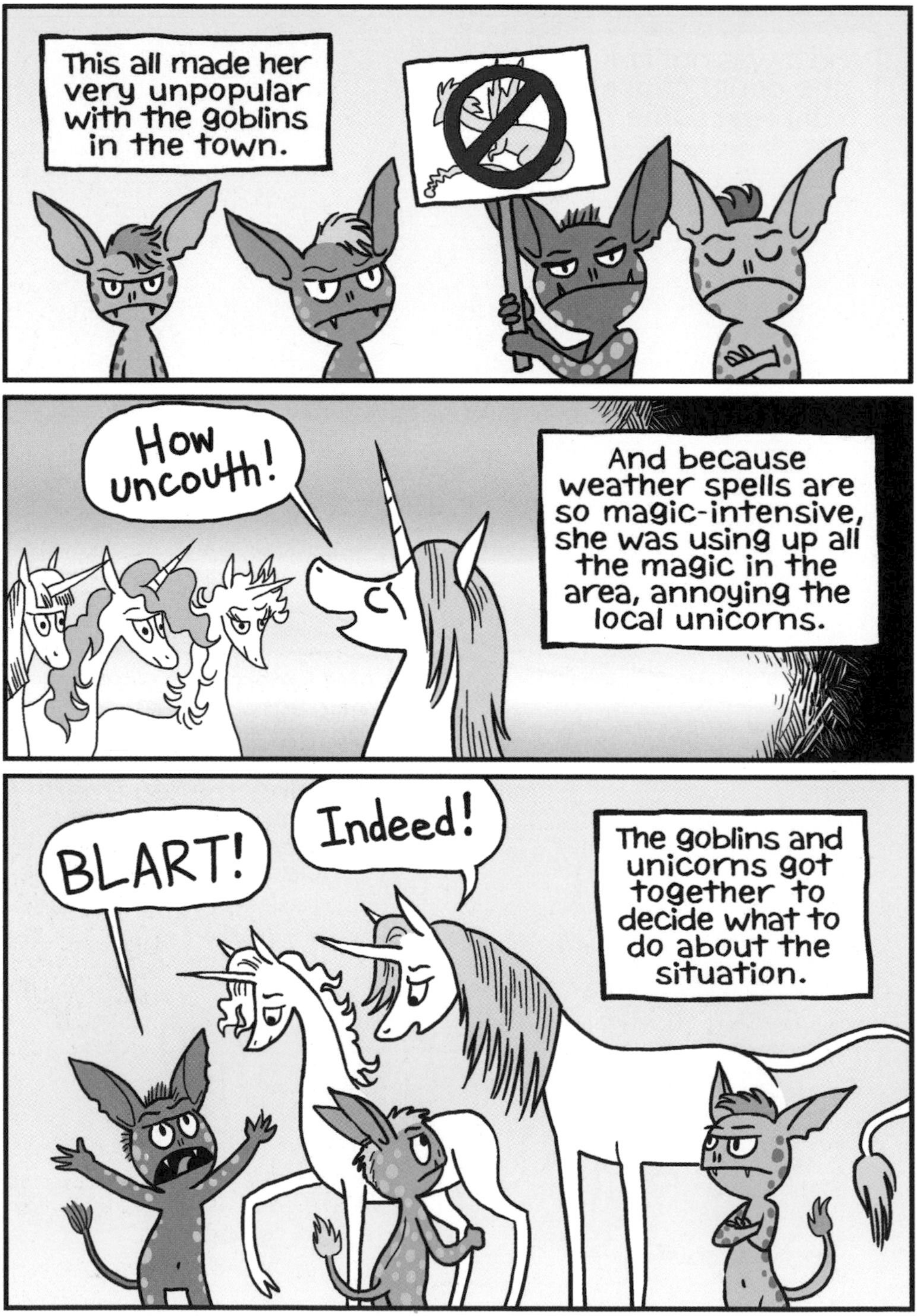
This all made her very unpopular with the goblins in the town.
How uncouth!
And because weather spells are so magic-intensive, she was using up all the magic in the area, annoying the local unicorns.
BLART!
Indeed!
The goblins and unicorns got together to decide what to do about the situation.

A
STERNLY WORDED PETITION.

79

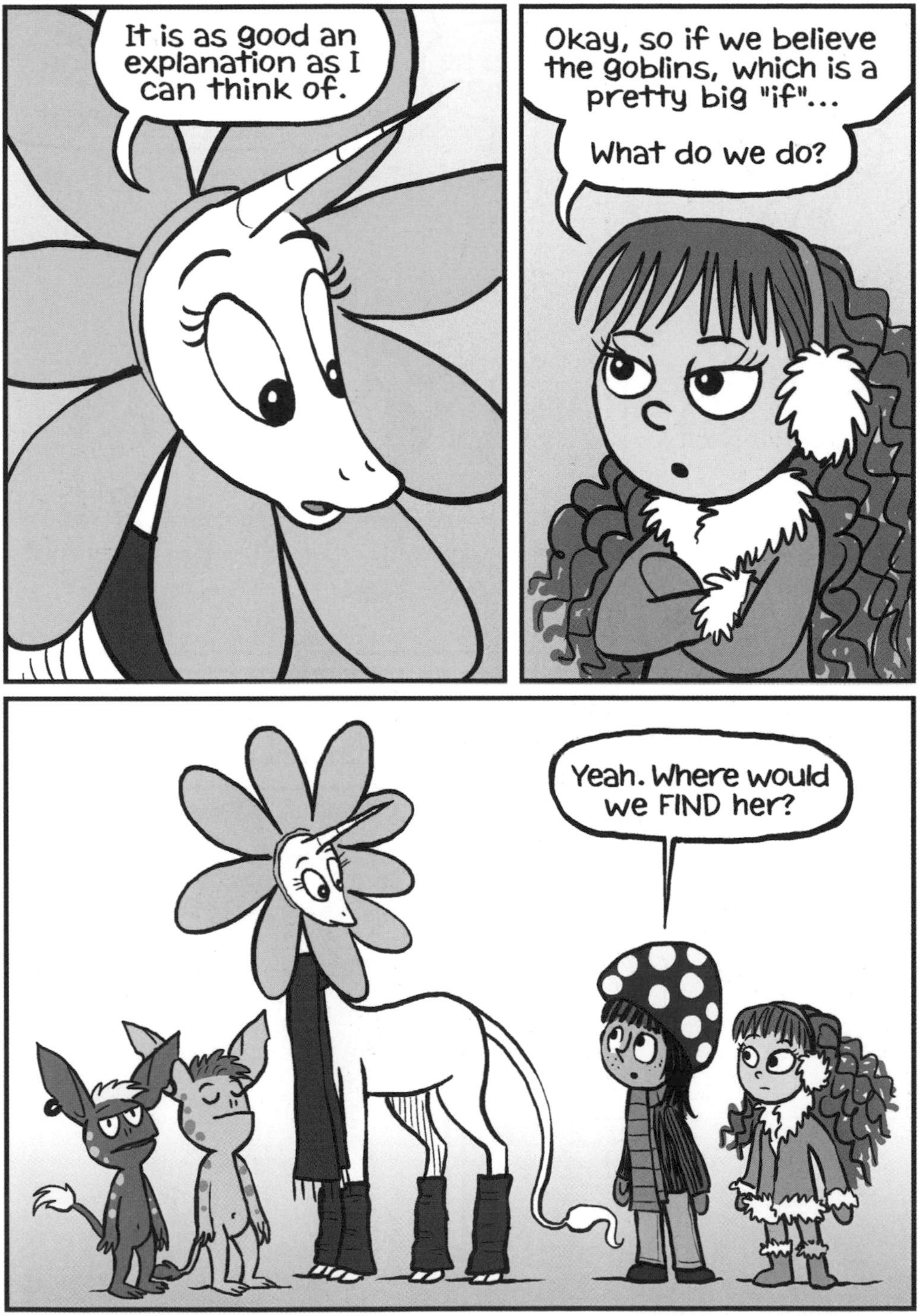
It is as good an explanation as I can think of.
Okay, so if we believe the goblins, which is a pretty big "if"...
What do we do?
Yeah. Where would we FIND her?

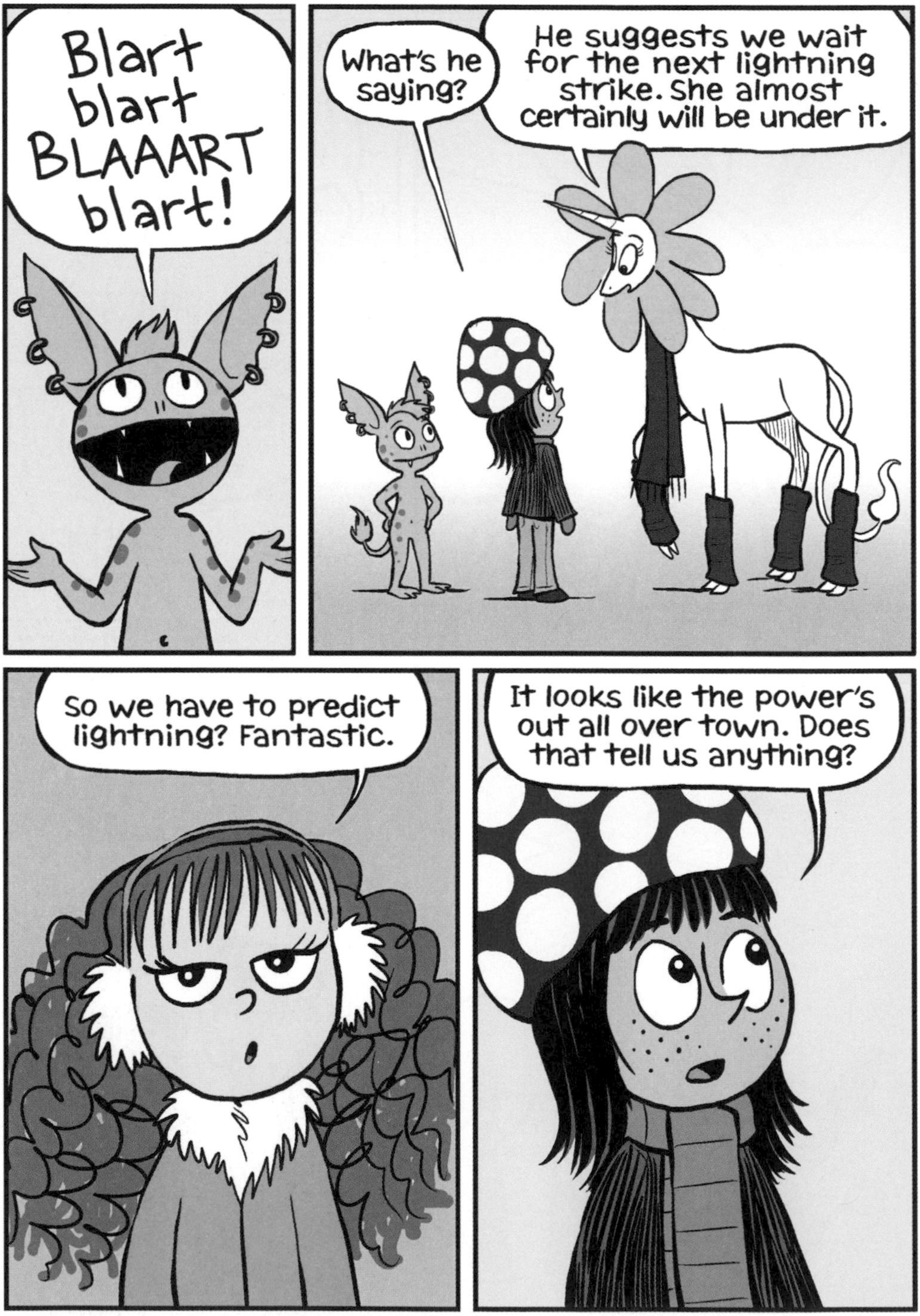
Blart blart BLAAART blart!
What's he saying?
He suggests we wait for the next lightning strike. She almost certainly will be under it.
So we have to predict lightning? Fantastic.
It looks like the power's out all over town. Does that tell us anything?

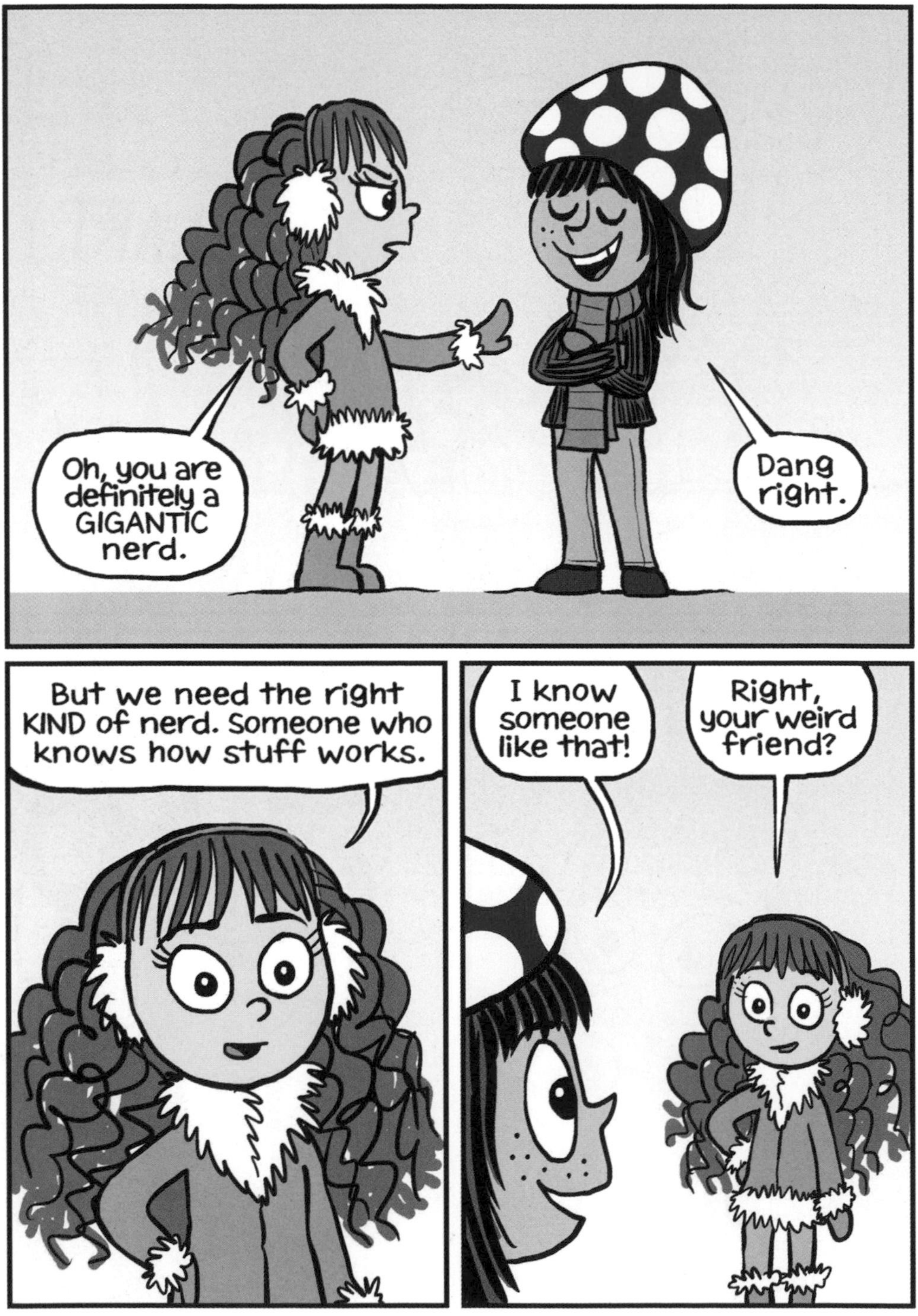
Oh, you are definitely a GIGANTIC nerd.
Dang right.
But we need the right KIND of nerd. Someone who knows how stuff works.
I know someone like that!
Right, your weird friend?

85

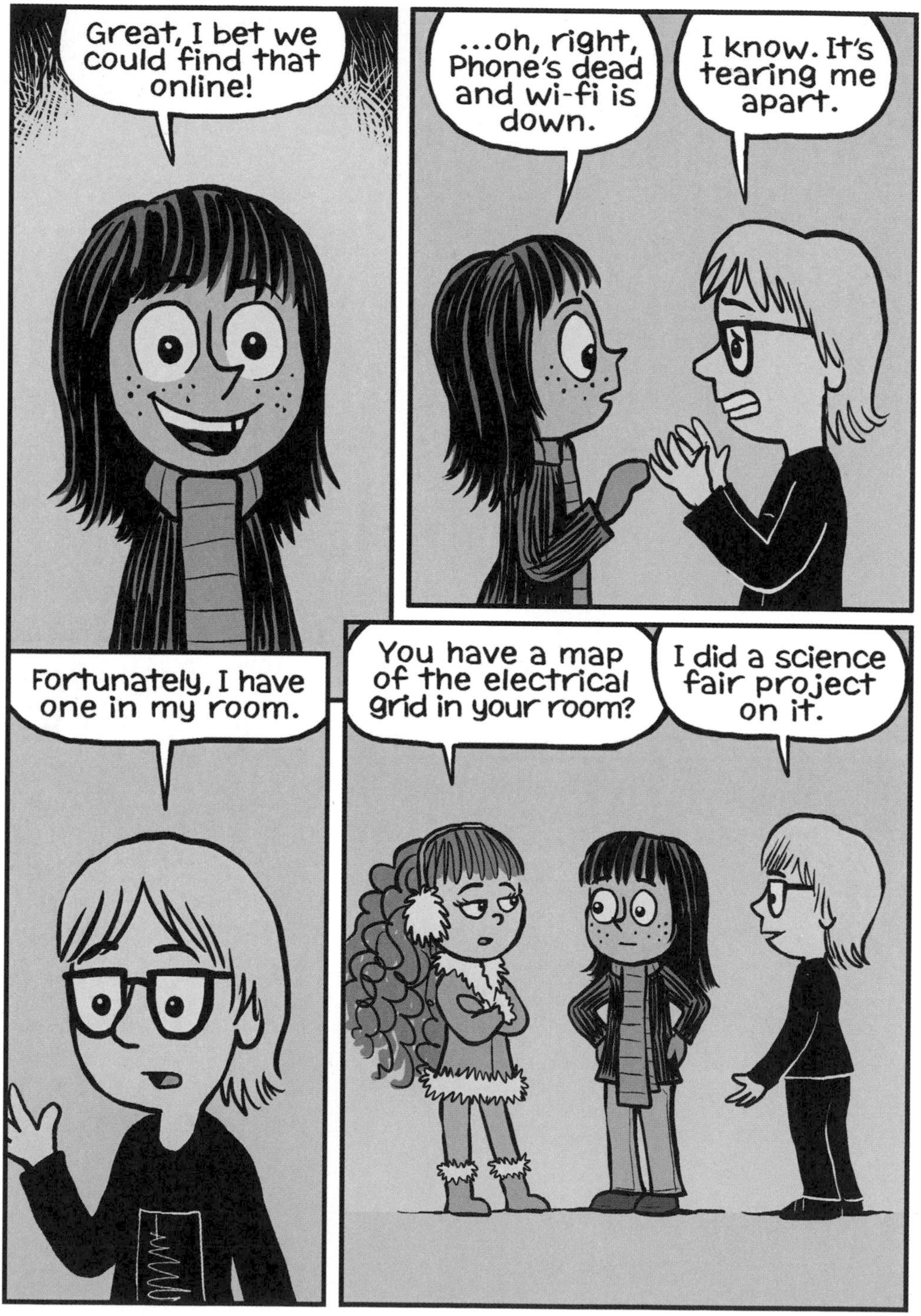
Great, I bet we could find that online!
...oh, right, Phone's dead and wi-fi is down.
I know. It's tearing me apart.
Fortunately, I have one in my room.
You have a map of the electrical grid in your room?
I did a science fair project on it.

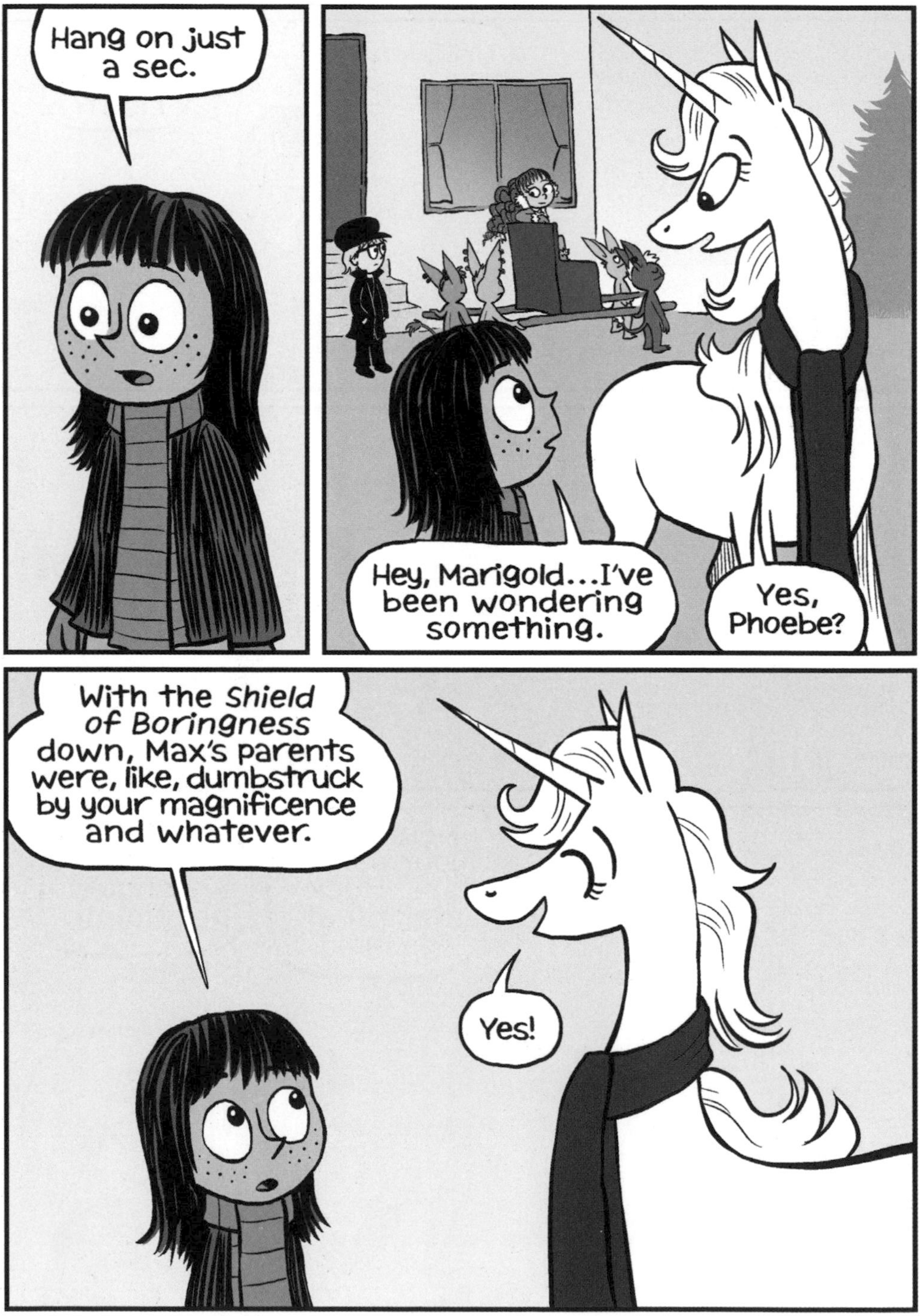
Hang on just a sec.
Hey, Marigold...I've been wondering something.
Yes, Phoebe?
With the *Shield of Boringness* down, Max's parents were, like, dumbstruck by your magnificence and whatever.
Yes!

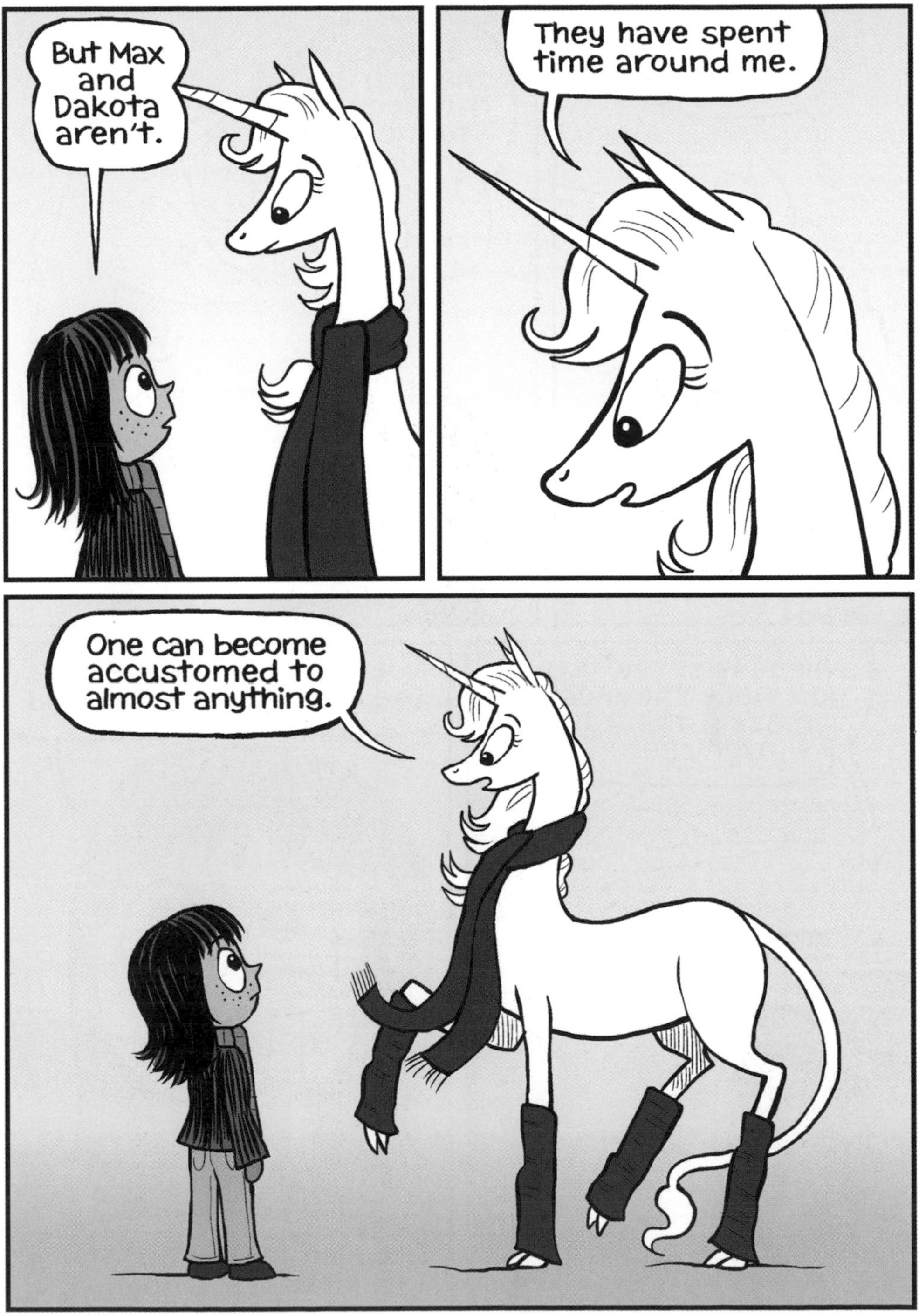
But Max and Dakota aren't.
They have spent time around me.
One can become accustomed to almost anything.

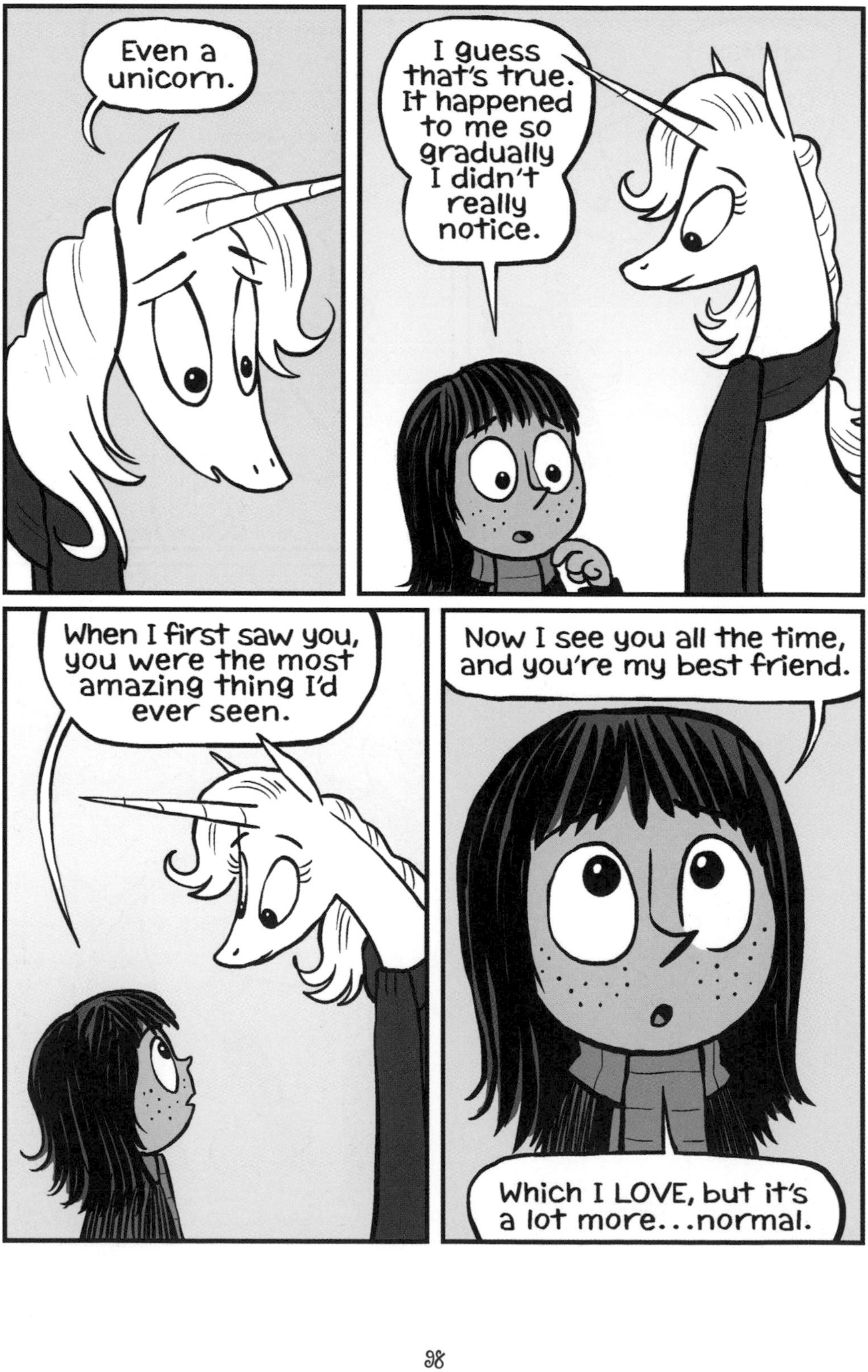
Even a unicorn.
I guess that's true. It happened to me so gradually I didn't really notice.
When I first saw you, you were the most amazing thing I'd ever seen.
Now I see you all the time, and you're my best friend.
Which I LOVE, but it's a lot more...normal.

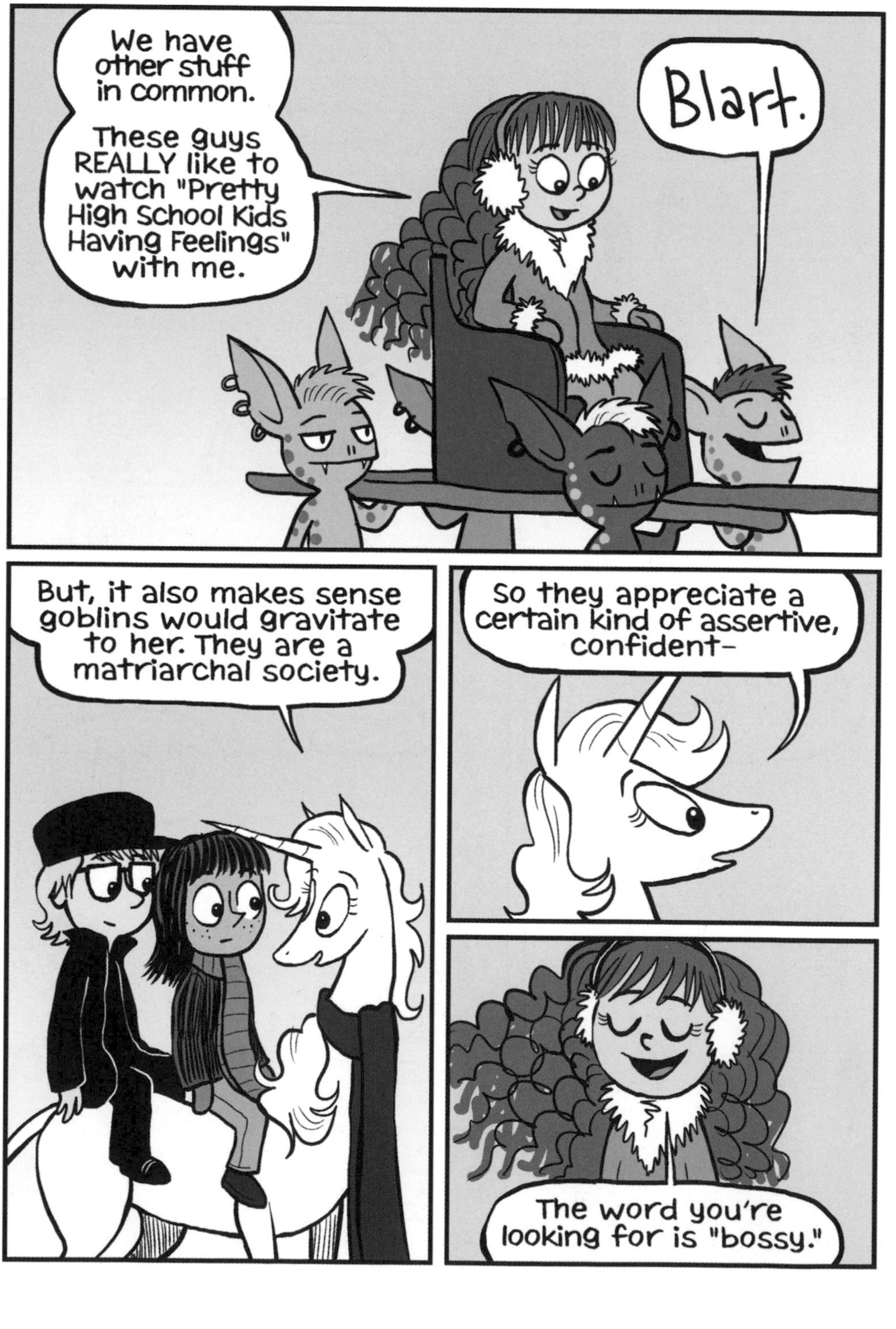
We have other stuff in common.
These guys REALLY like to watch "Pretty High School Kids Having Feelings" with me.
Blart.
But, it also makes sense goblins would gravitate to her. They are a matriarchal society.
So they appreciate a certain kind of assertive, confident-
The word you're looking for is "bossy."

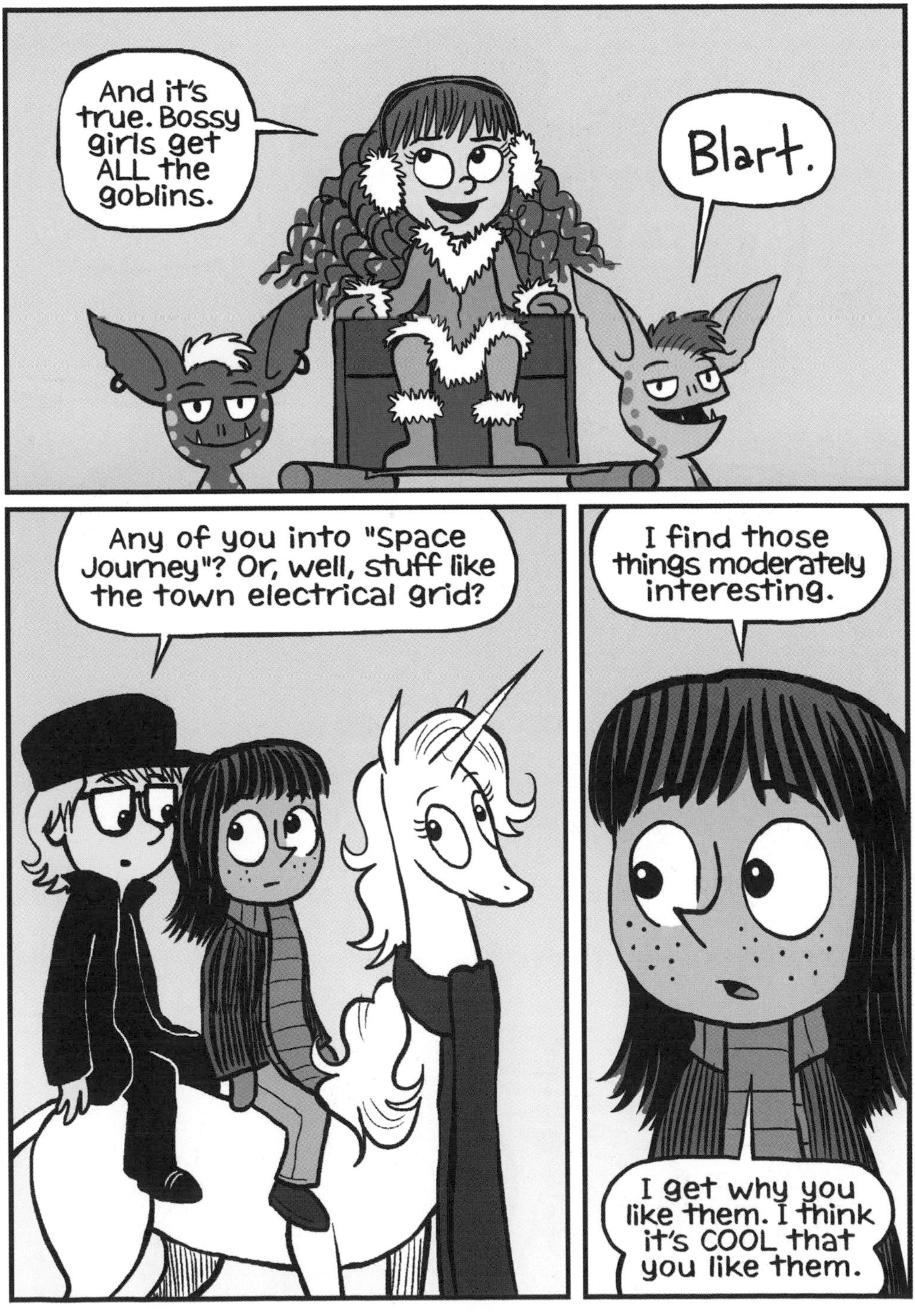
And it's true. Bossy girls get ALL the goblins.
Blart.
Any of you into "Space Journey"? Or, well, stuff like the town electrical grid?
I find those things moderately interesting.
I get why you like them. I think it's COOL that you like them.

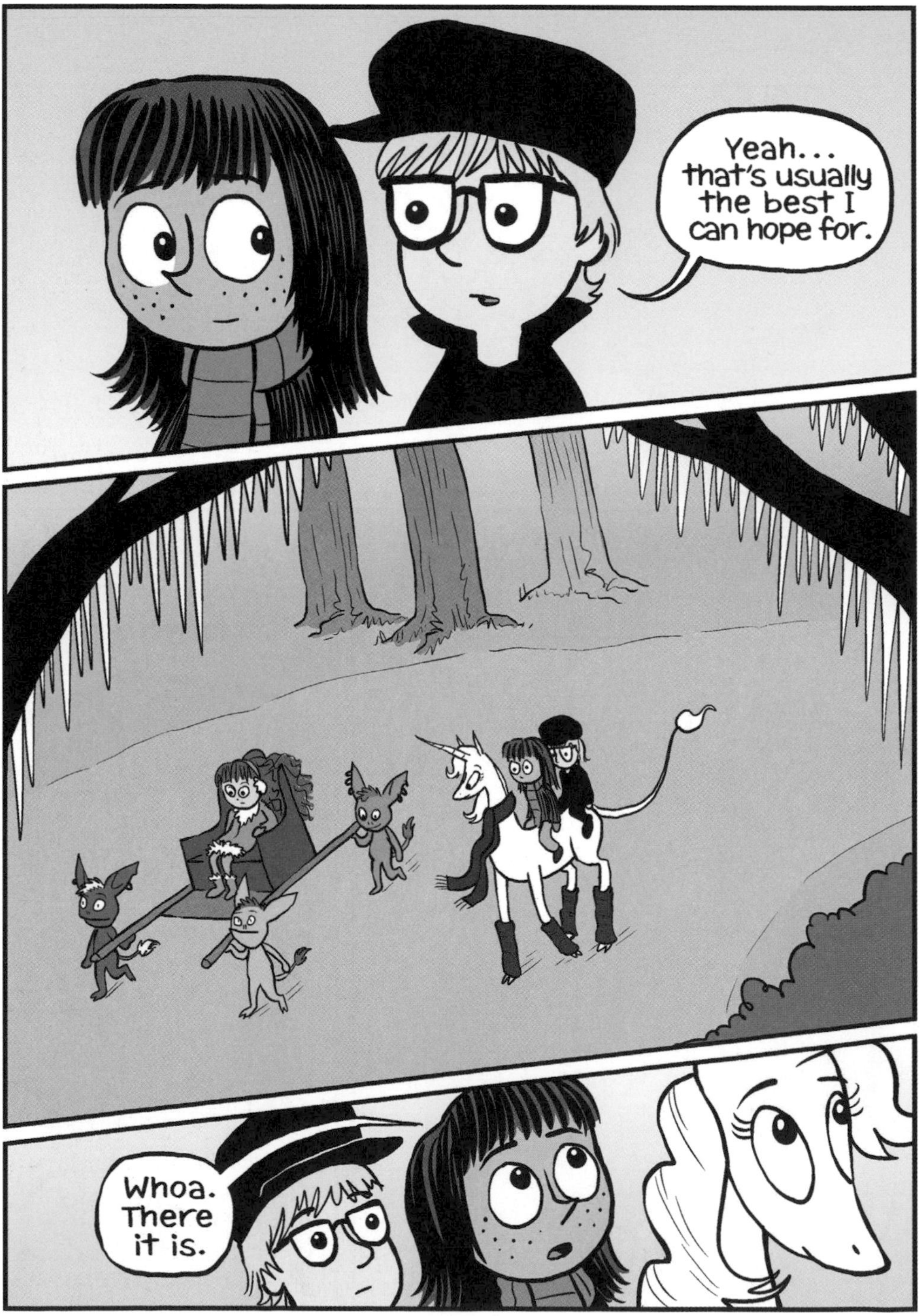
Yeah... that's usually the best I can hope for.
Whoa. There it is.

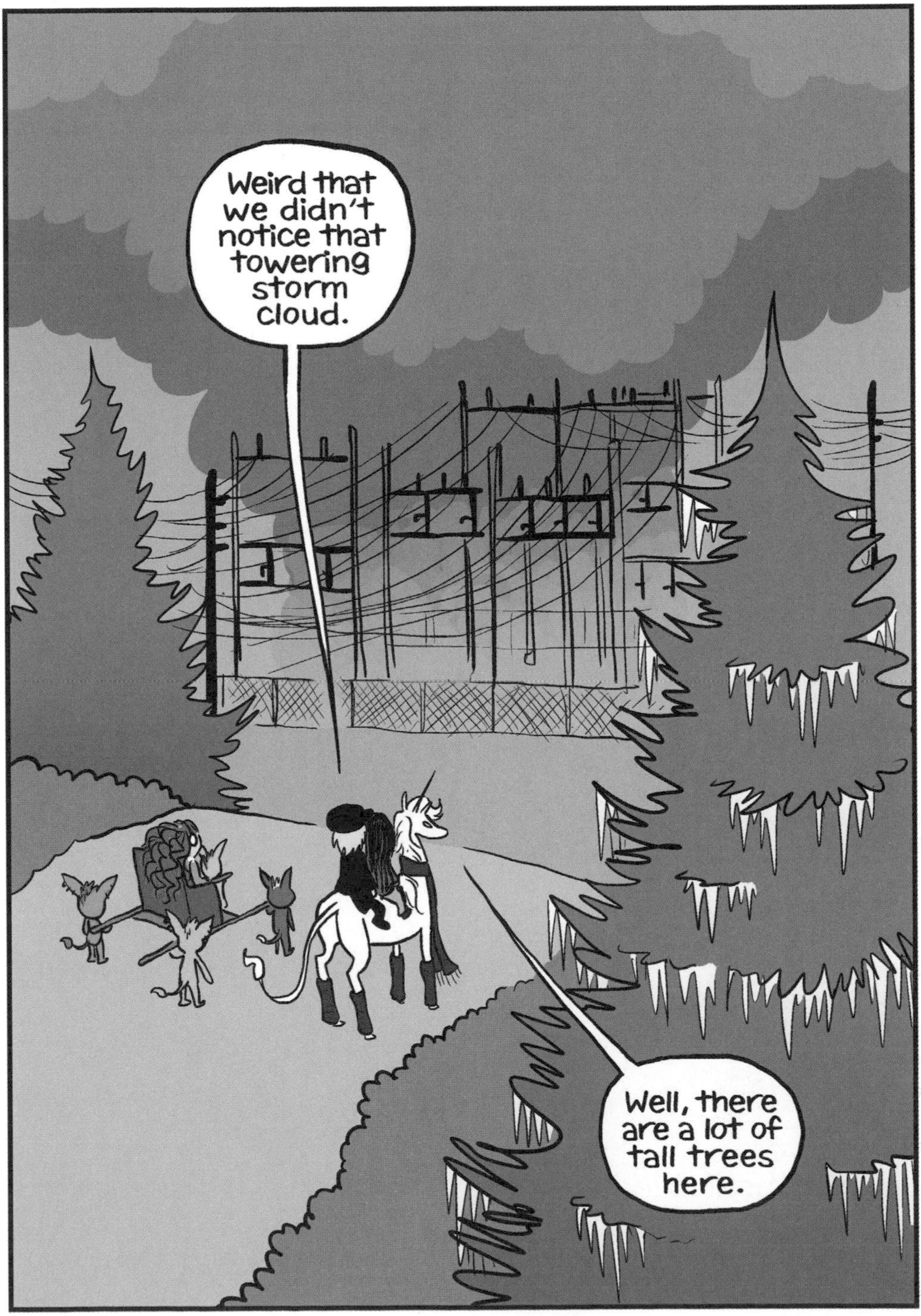
Weird that we didn't notice that towering storm cloud.
Well, there are a lot of tall trees here.

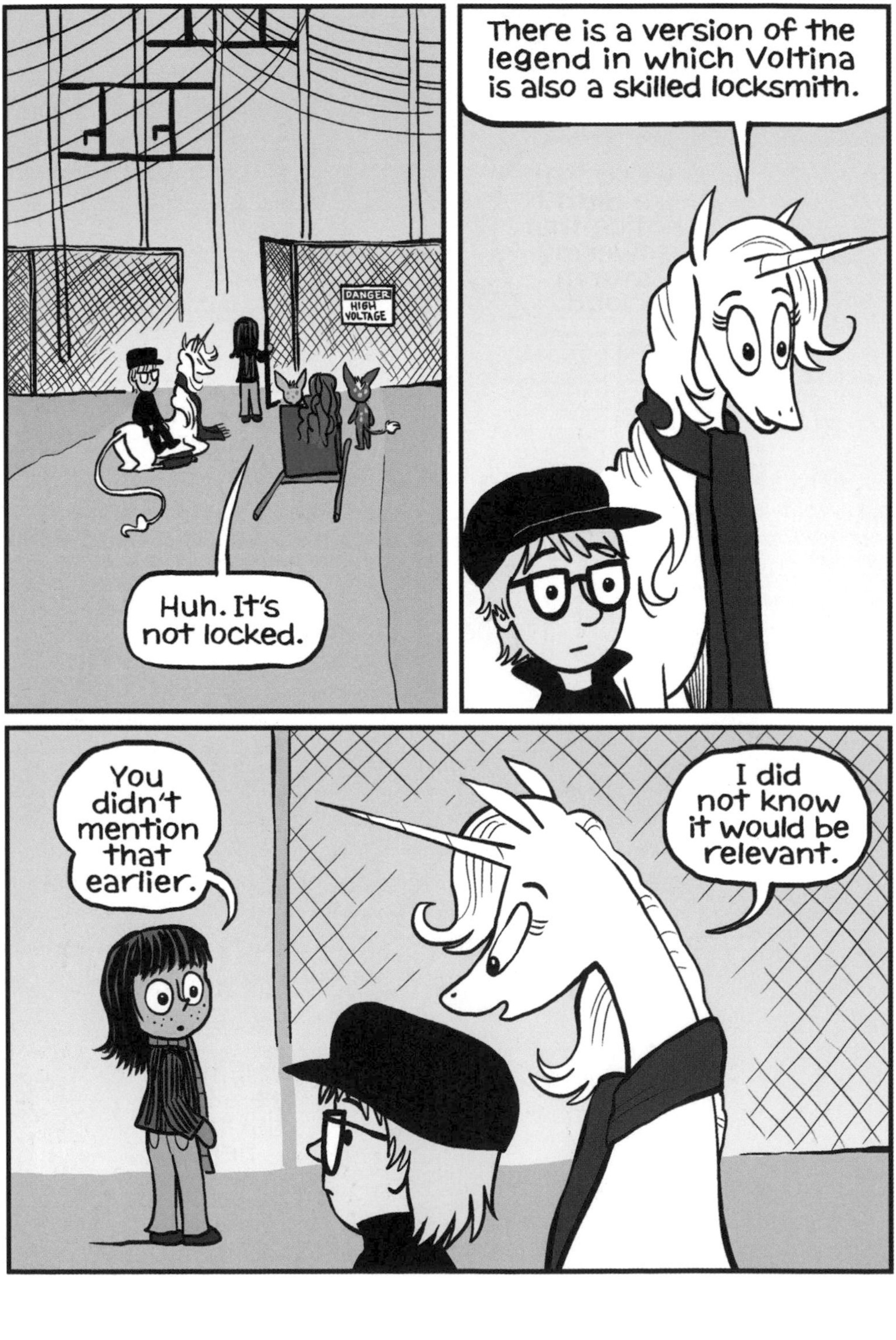
DANGER
HIGH VOLTAGE
Huh. It's not locked.
There is a version of the legend in which Voltina is also a skilled locksmith.
You didn't mention that earlier.
I did not know it would be relevant.

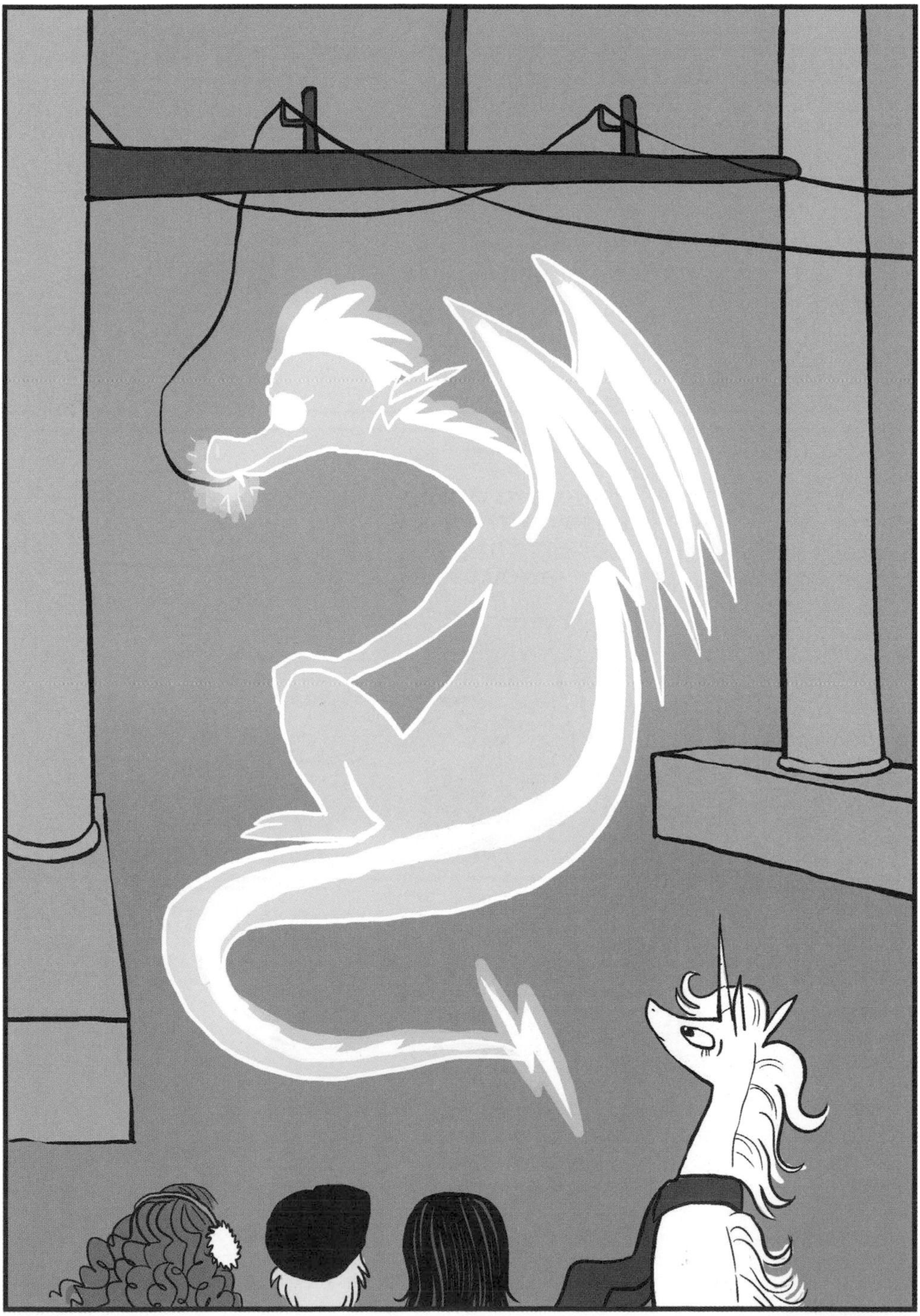

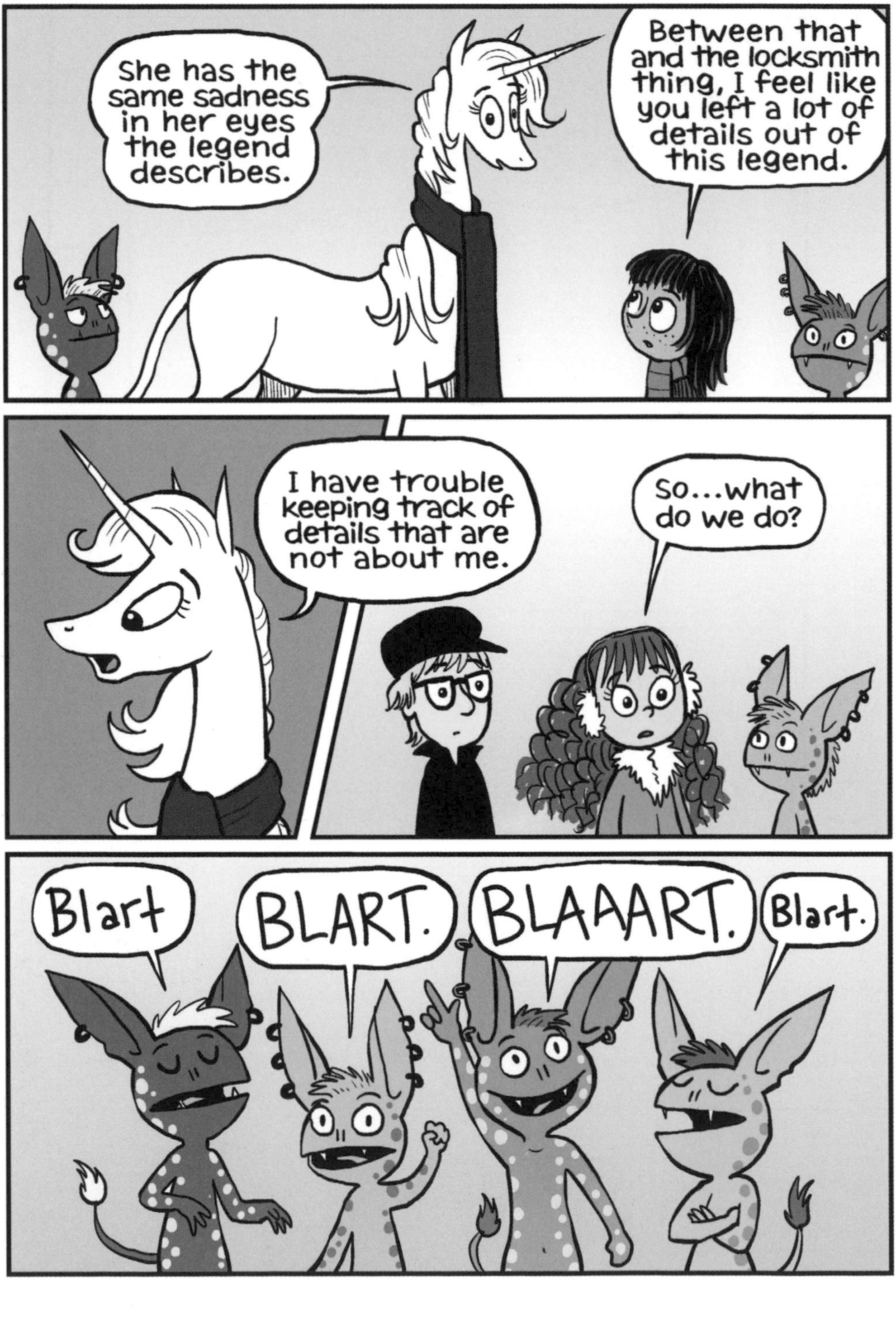
She has the same sadness in her eyes the legend describes.
Between that and the locksmith thing, I feel like you left a lot of details out of this legend.
I have trouble keeping track of details that are not about me.
So...what do we do?
Blart
BLART.
BLAAART.
Blart.

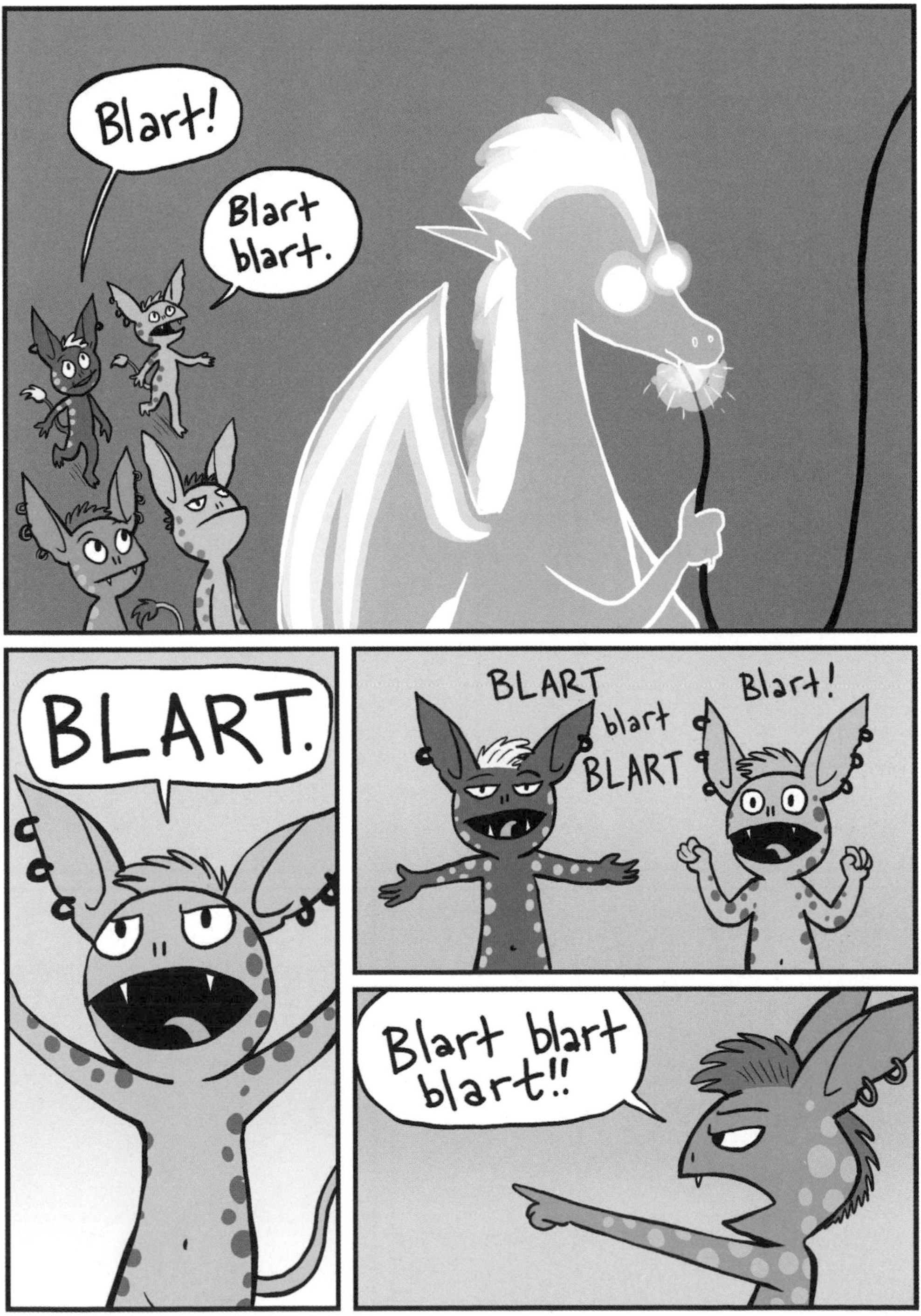
Blart!
Blart blart.
BLART.
BLART
blart
BLART
Blart!
Blart blart blart!!

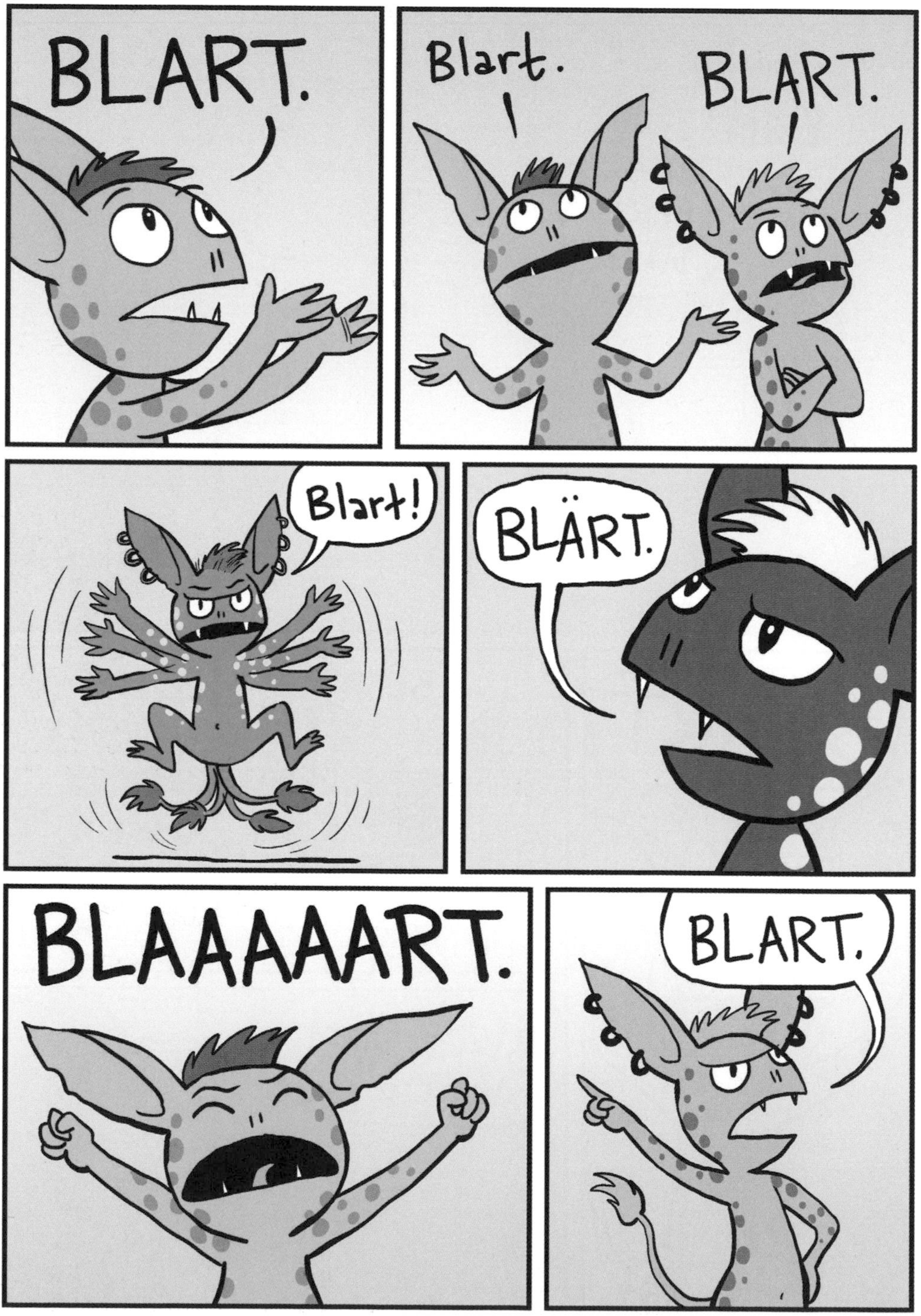
BLART.
Blart.
BLART.
Blart!
BLÄRT.
BLAAAAART.
BLART.

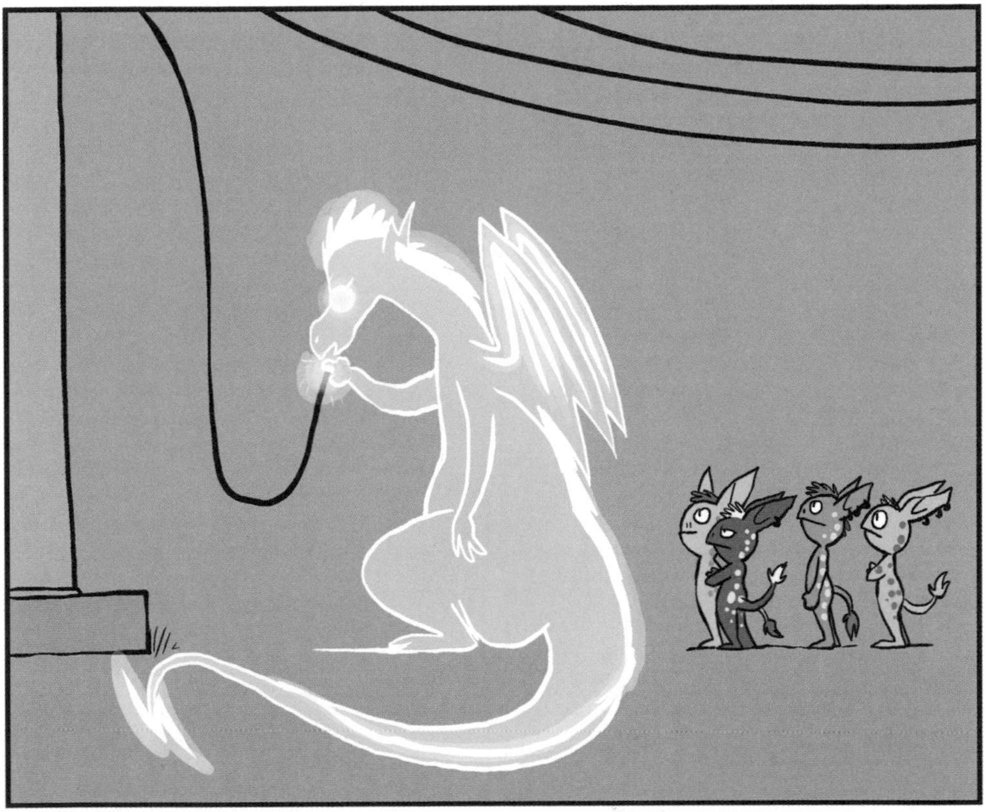

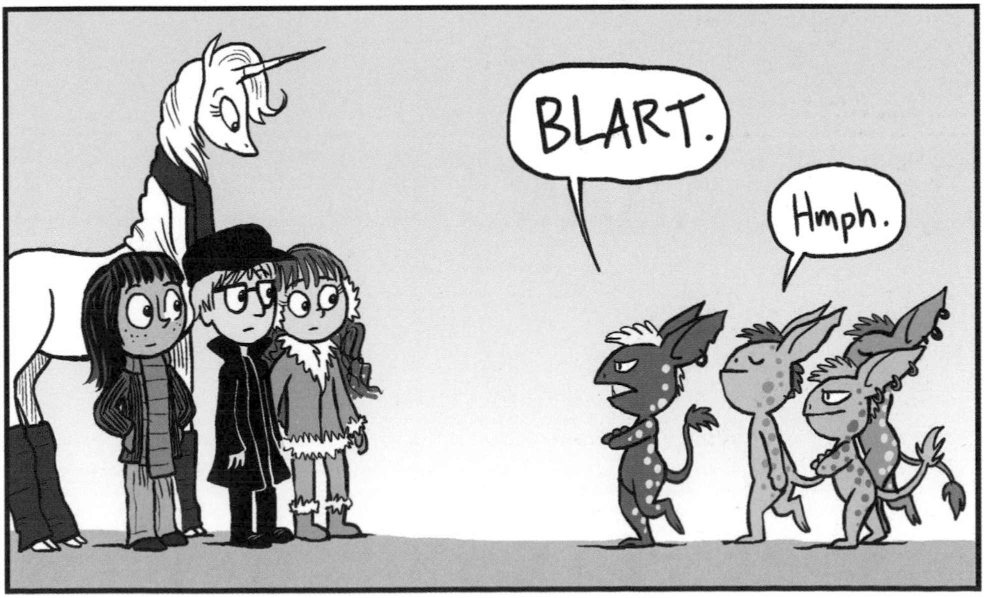
BLART.
Hmph.

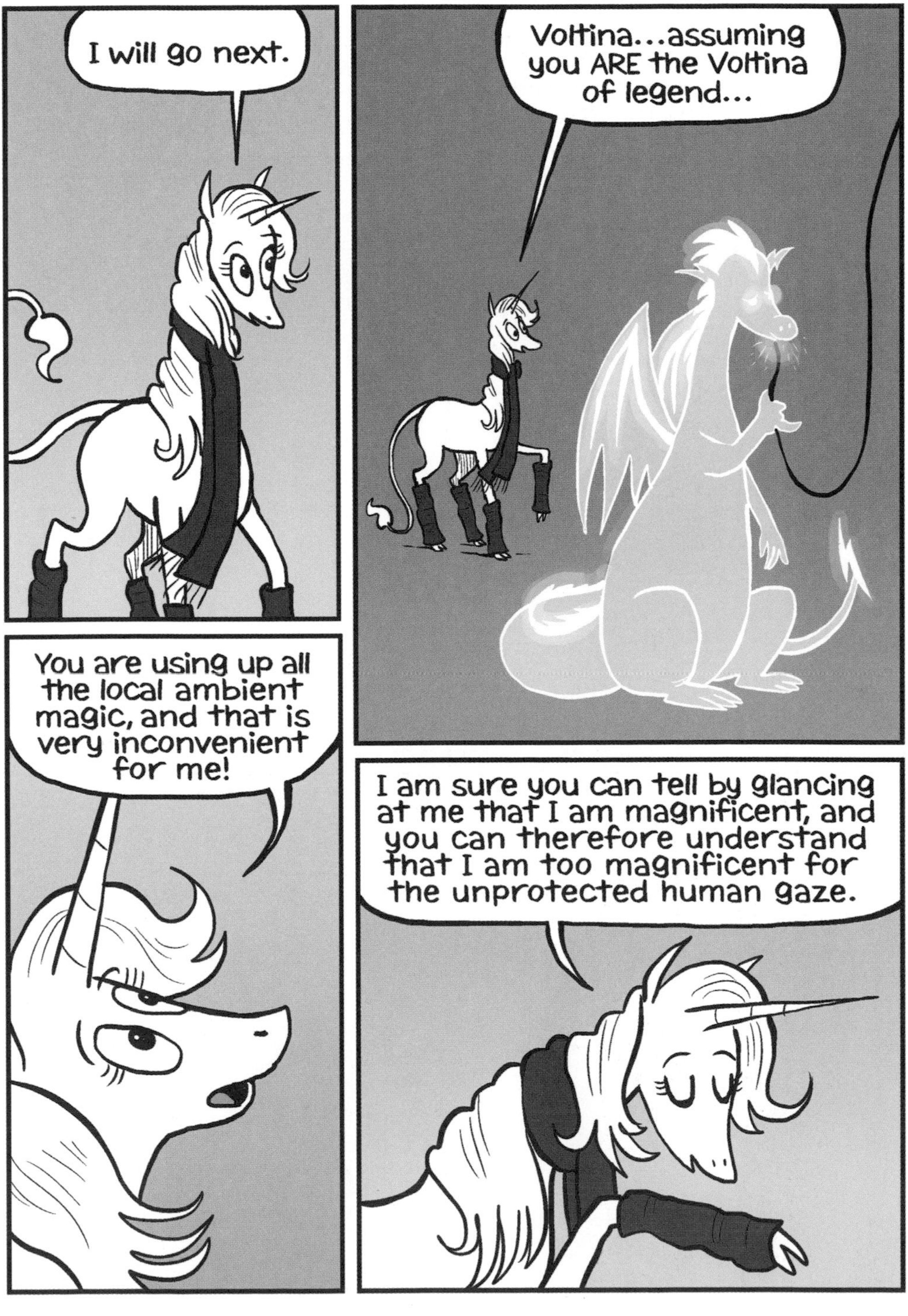
I will go next.
Voltina...assuming you ARE the Voltina of legend...
You are using up all the local ambient magic, and that is very inconvenient for me!
I am sure you can tell by glancing at me that I am magnificent, and you can therefore understand that I am too magnificent for the unprotected human gaze.

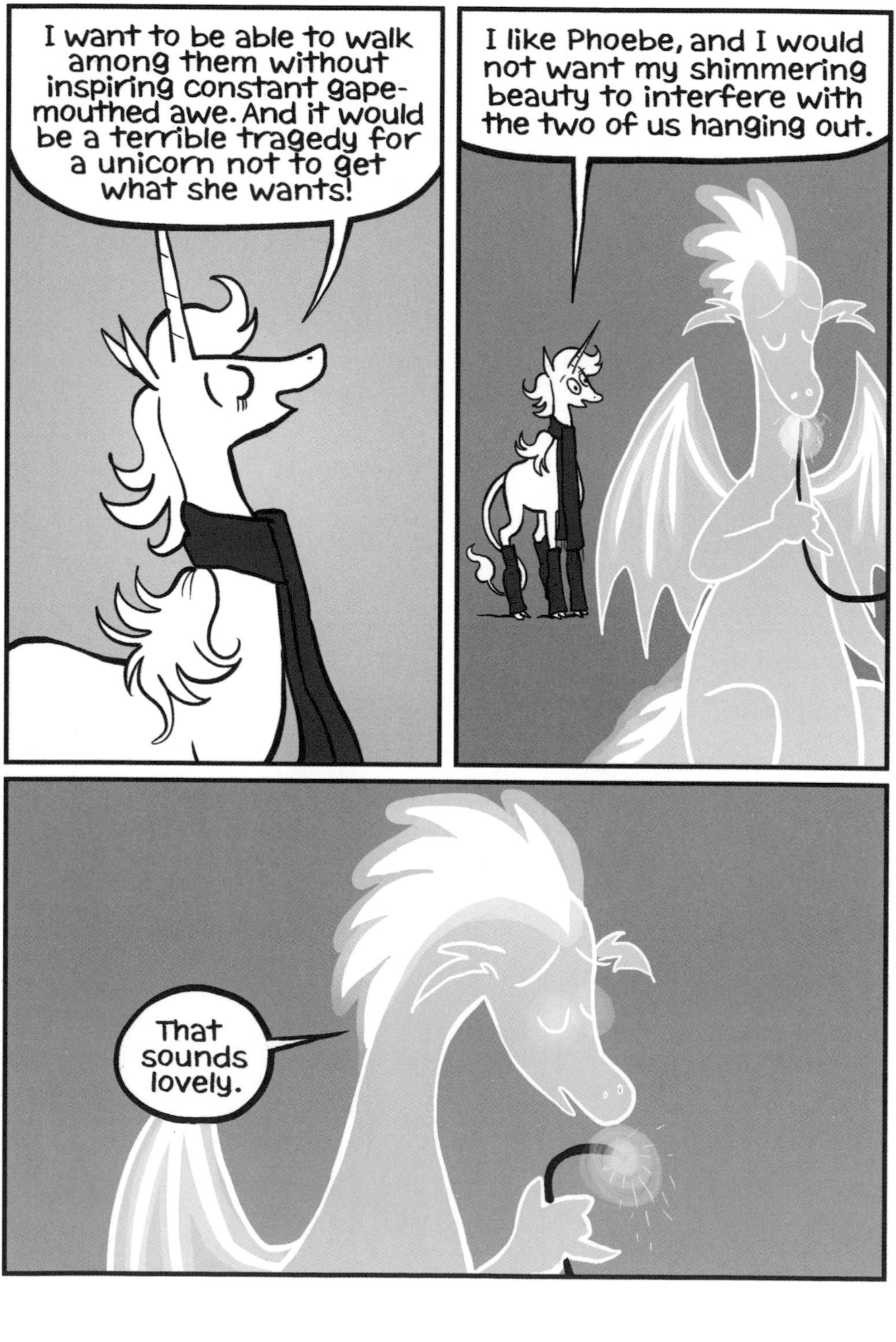
I want to be able to walk among them without inspiring constant gape-mouthed awe. And it would be a terrible tragedy for a unicorn not to get what she wants!
I like Phoebe, and I would not want my shimmering beauty to interfere with the two of us hanging out.
That sounds lovely.

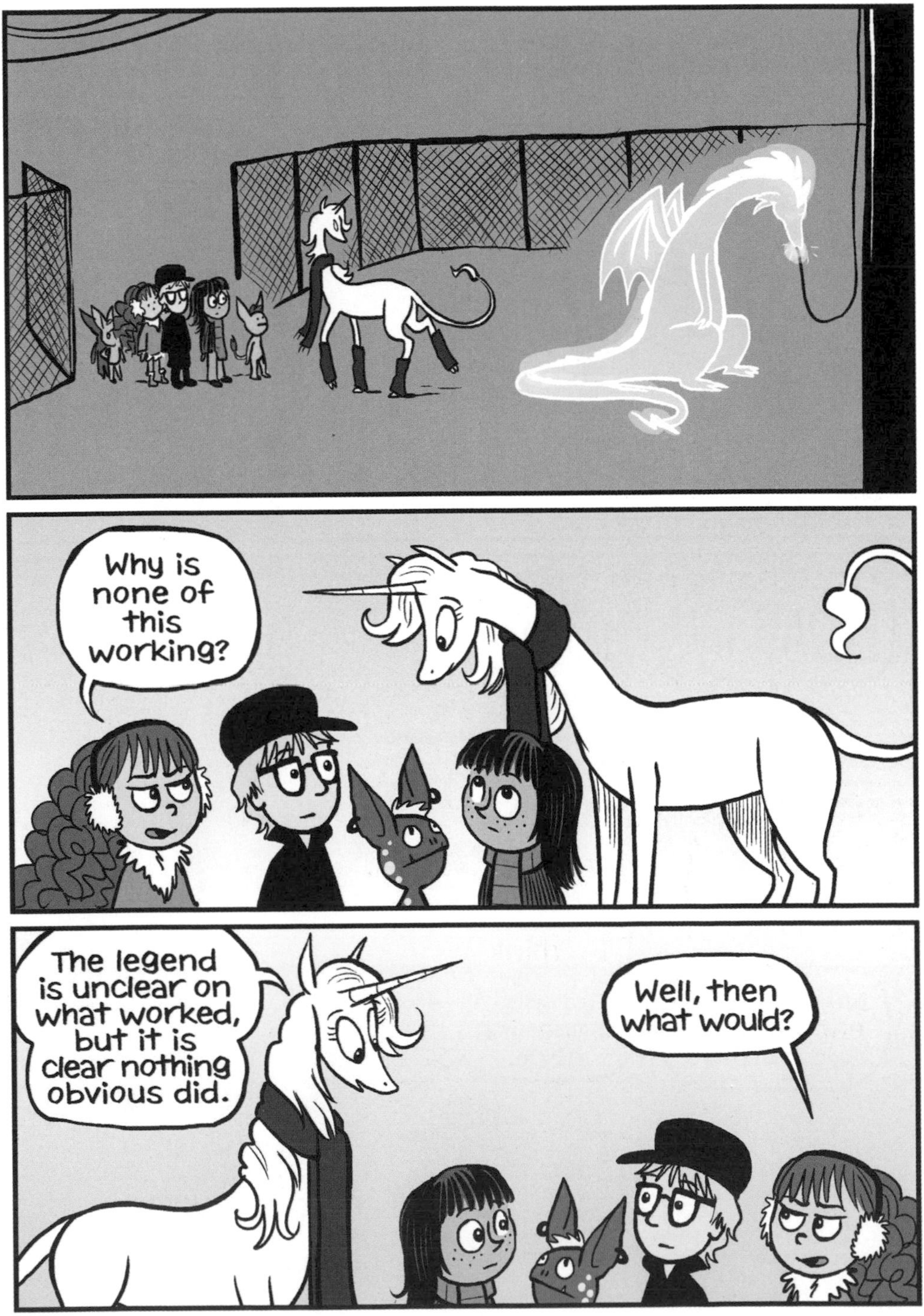
Why is none of this working?
The legend is unclear on what worked, but it is clear nothing obvious did.
Well, then what would?

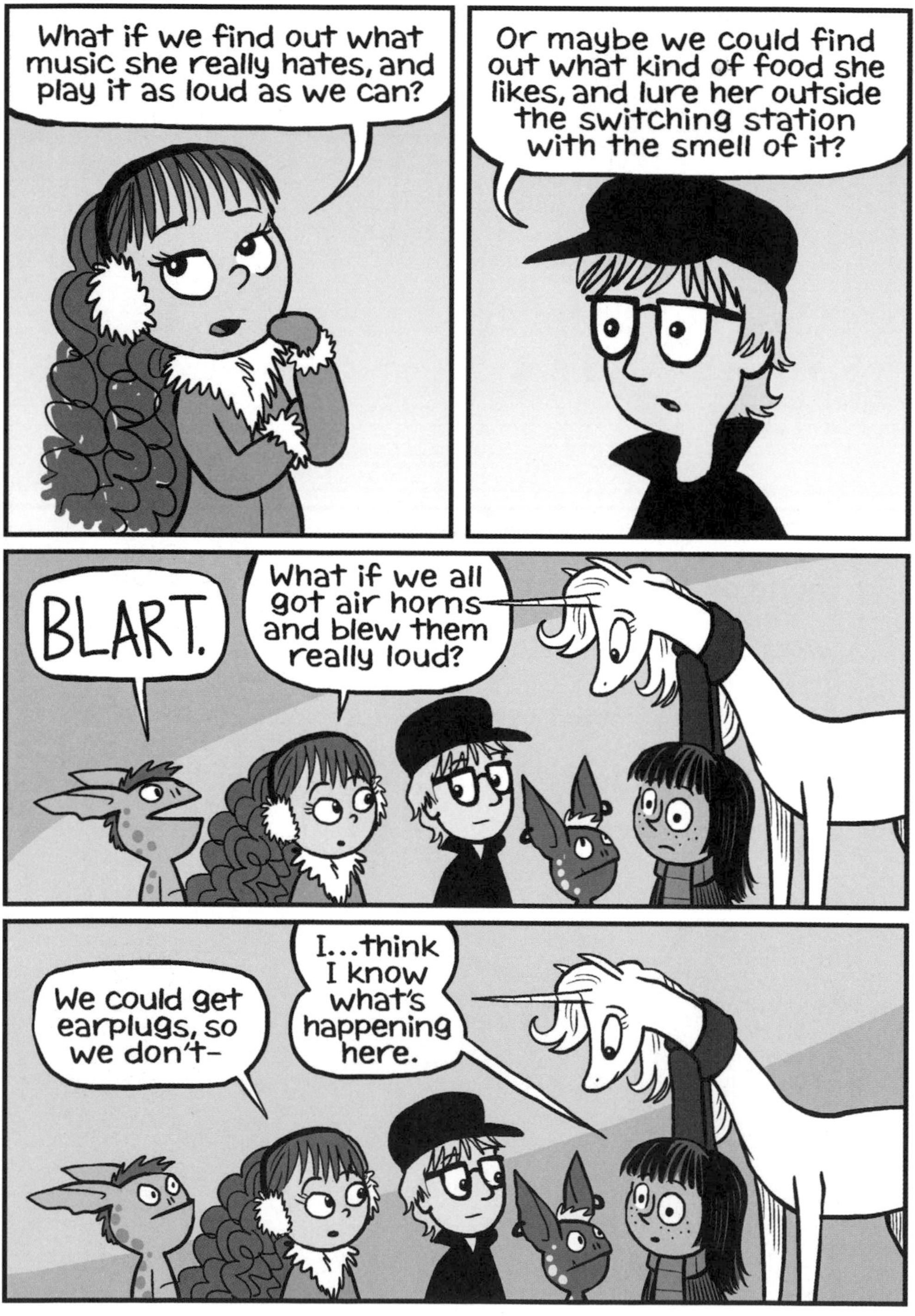
What if we find out what music she really hates, and play it as loud as we can?
Or maybe we could find out what kind of food she likes, and lure her outside the switching station with the smell of it?
BLART.
What if we all got air horns and blew them really loud?
We could get earplugs, so we don't-
I...think I know what's happening here.

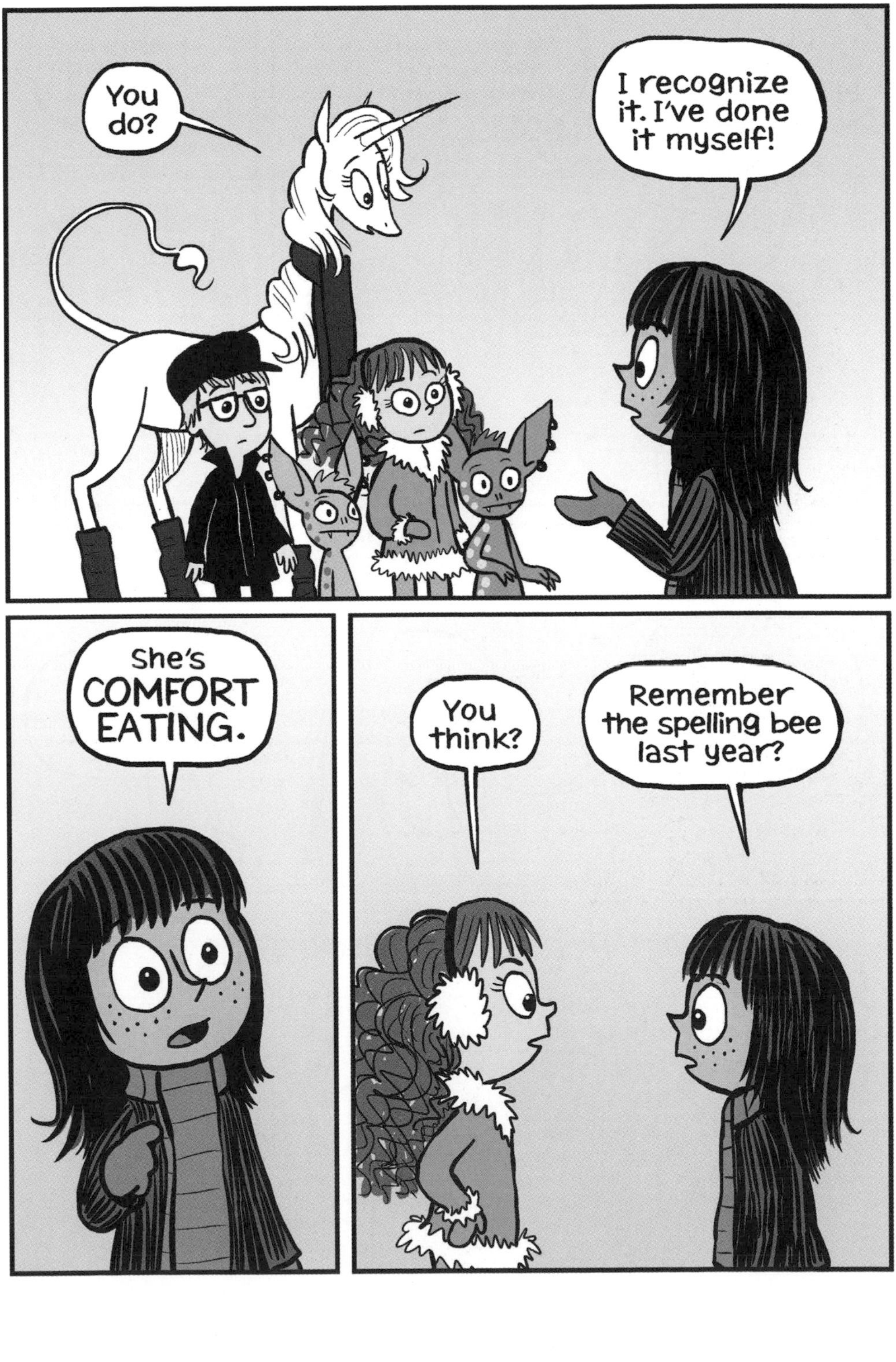
You do?
I recognize it. I've done it myself!
She's COMFORT EATING.
You think?
Remember the spelling bee last year?

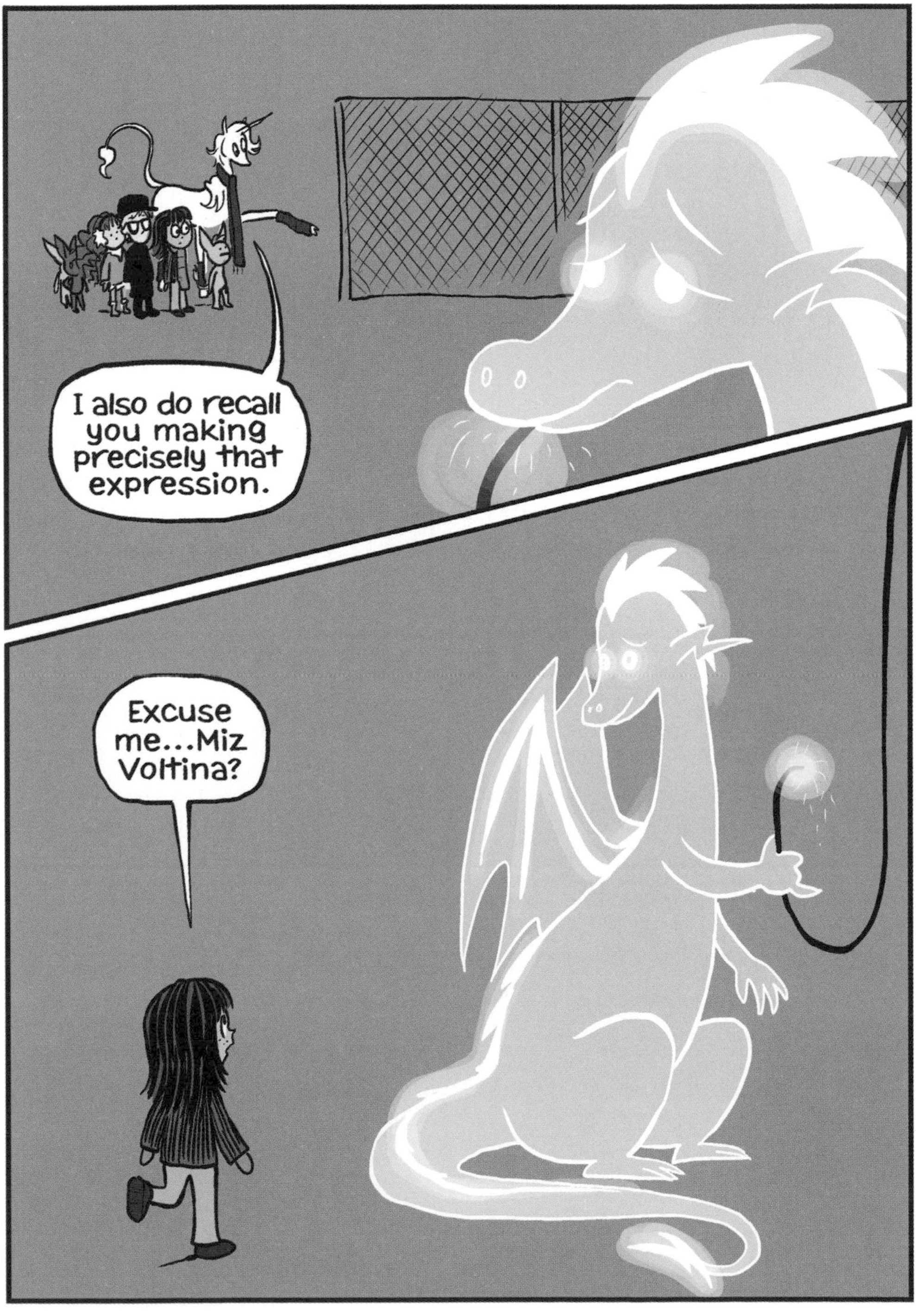
I also do recall you making precisely that expression.
Excuse me...Miz Voltina?

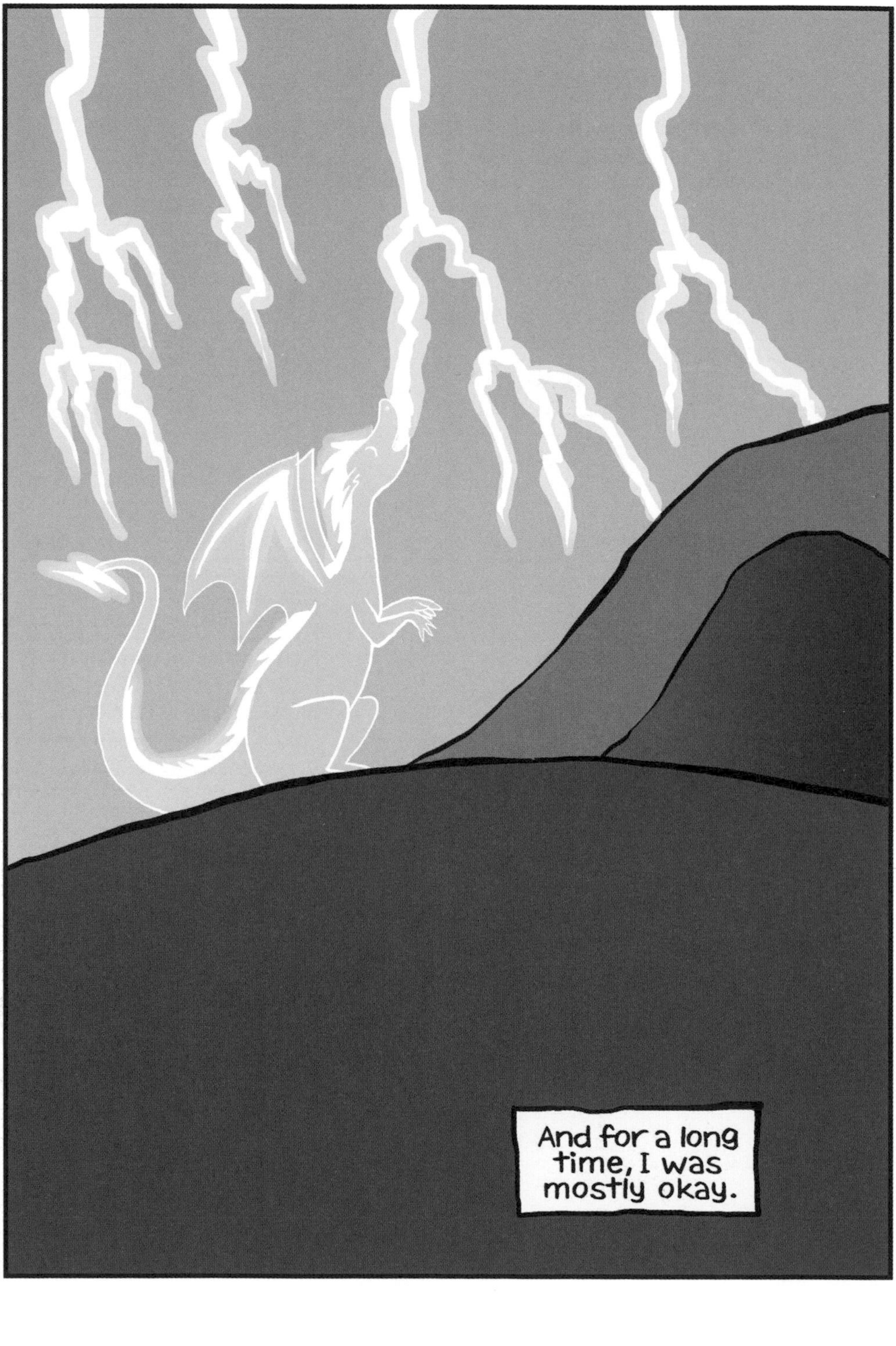
And for a long time, I was mostly okay.

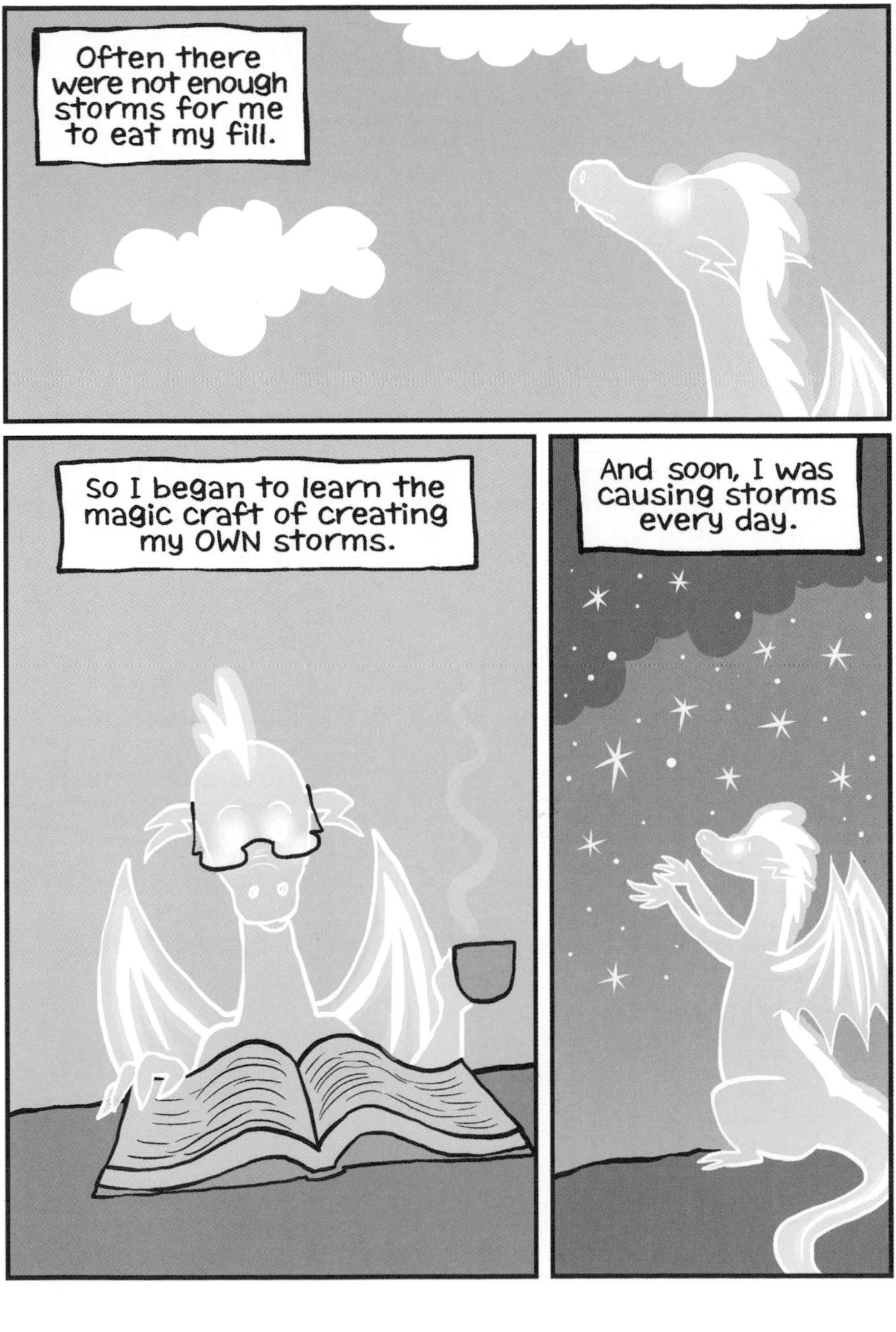
Often there were not enough storms for me to eat my fill.
So I began to learn the magic craft of creating my OWN storms.
And soon, I was causing storms every day.

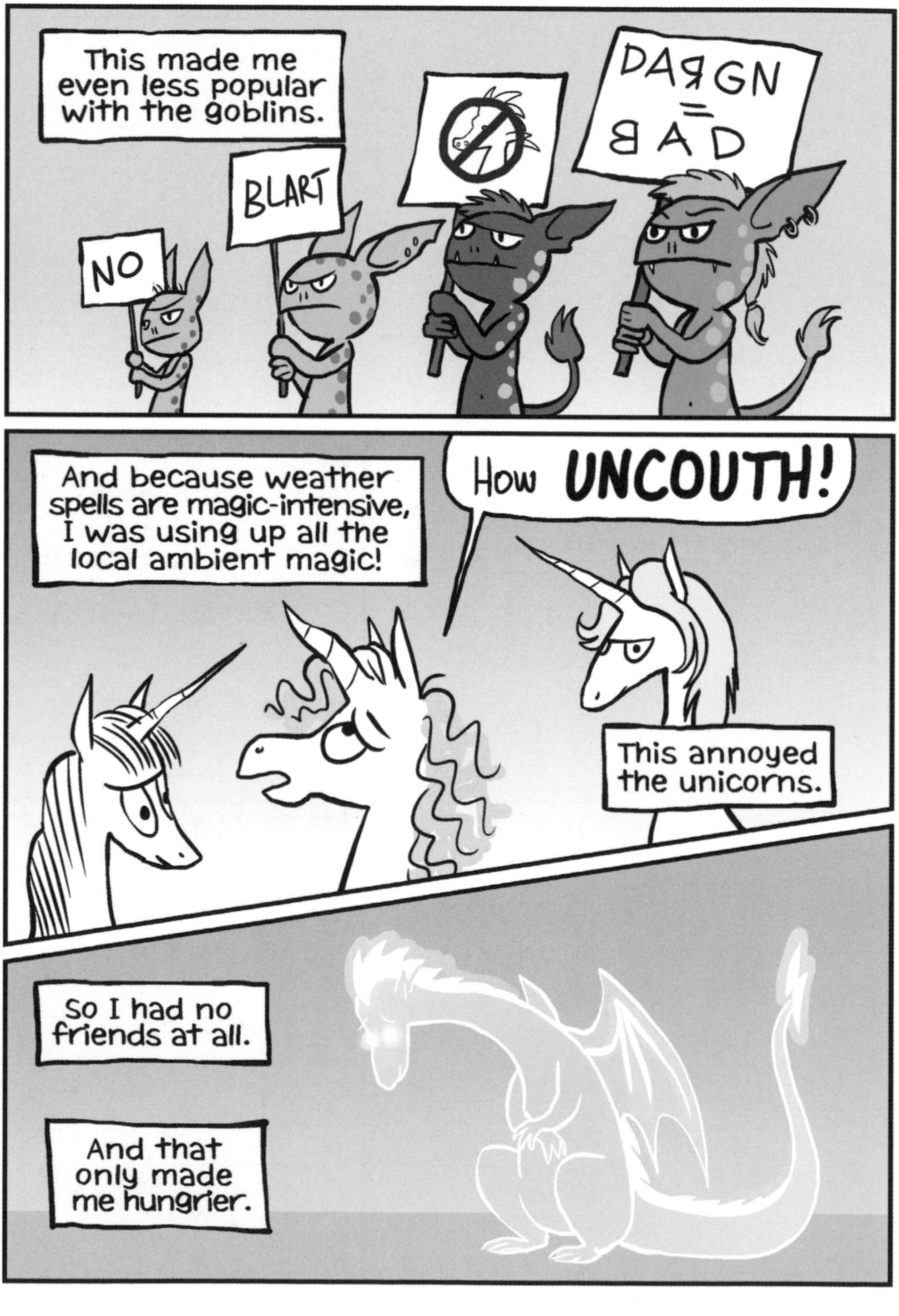
This made me even less popular with the goblins.
NO
BLART
DARGN = BAD
And because weather spells are magic-intensive, I was using up all the local ambient magic!
How UNCOUTH!
This annoyed the unicorns.
So I had no friends at all.
And that only made me hungrier.

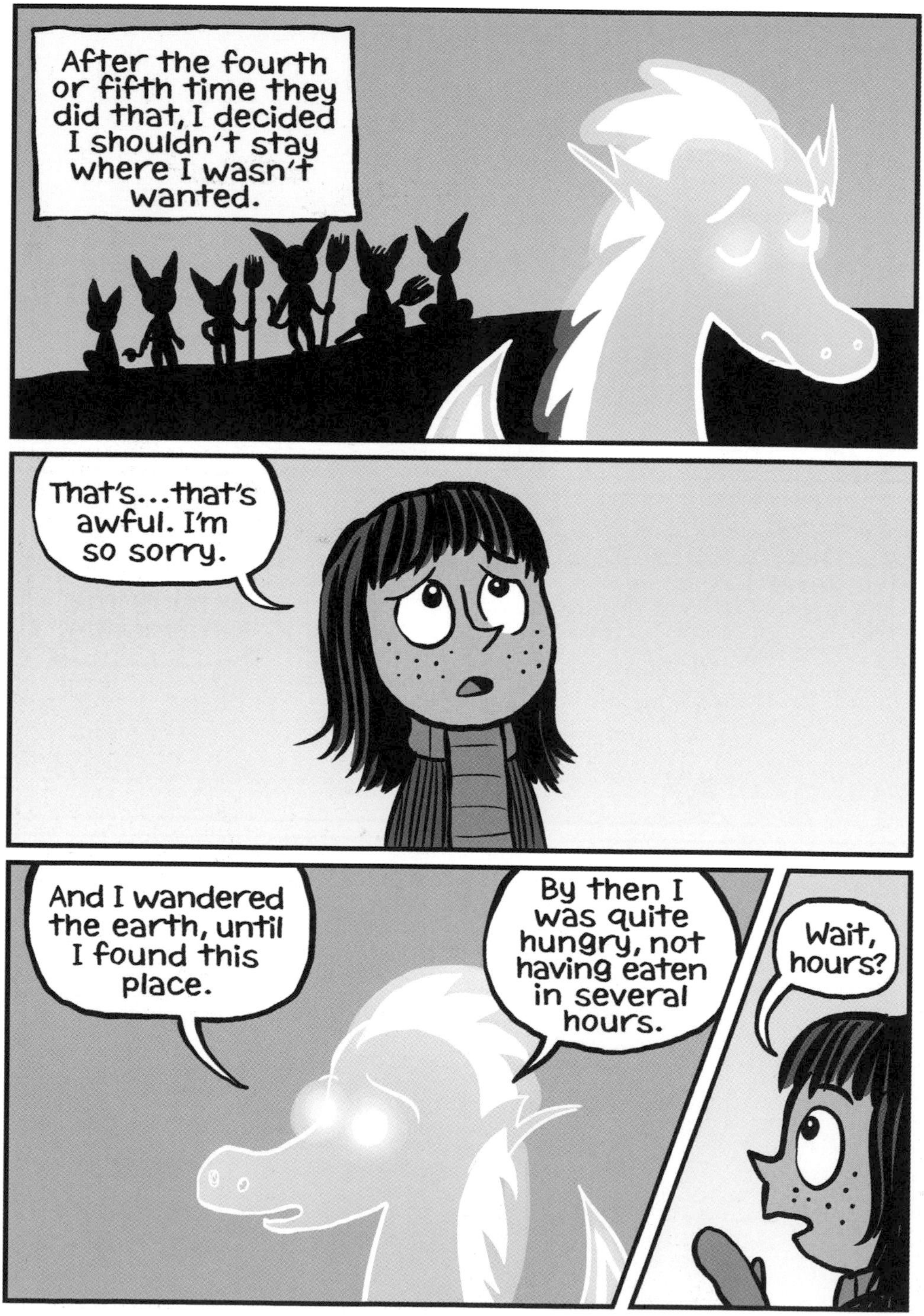
After the fourth or fifth time they did that, I decided I shouldn't stay where I wasn't wanted.
That's...that's awful. I'm so sorry.
And I wandered the earth, until I found this place.
By then I was quite hungry, not having eaten in several hours.
Wait, hours?

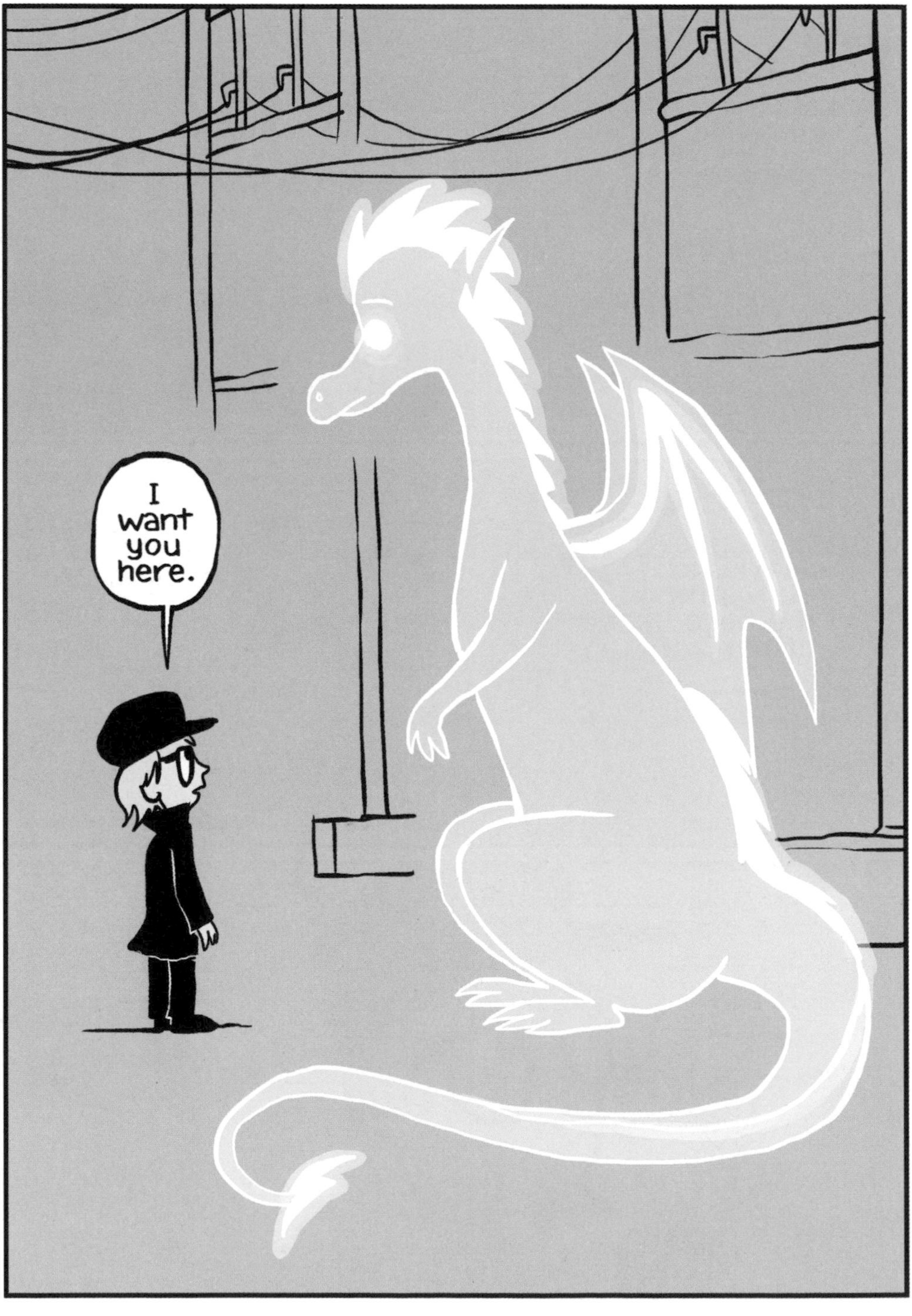
I want you here.

THREE MONTHS LATER

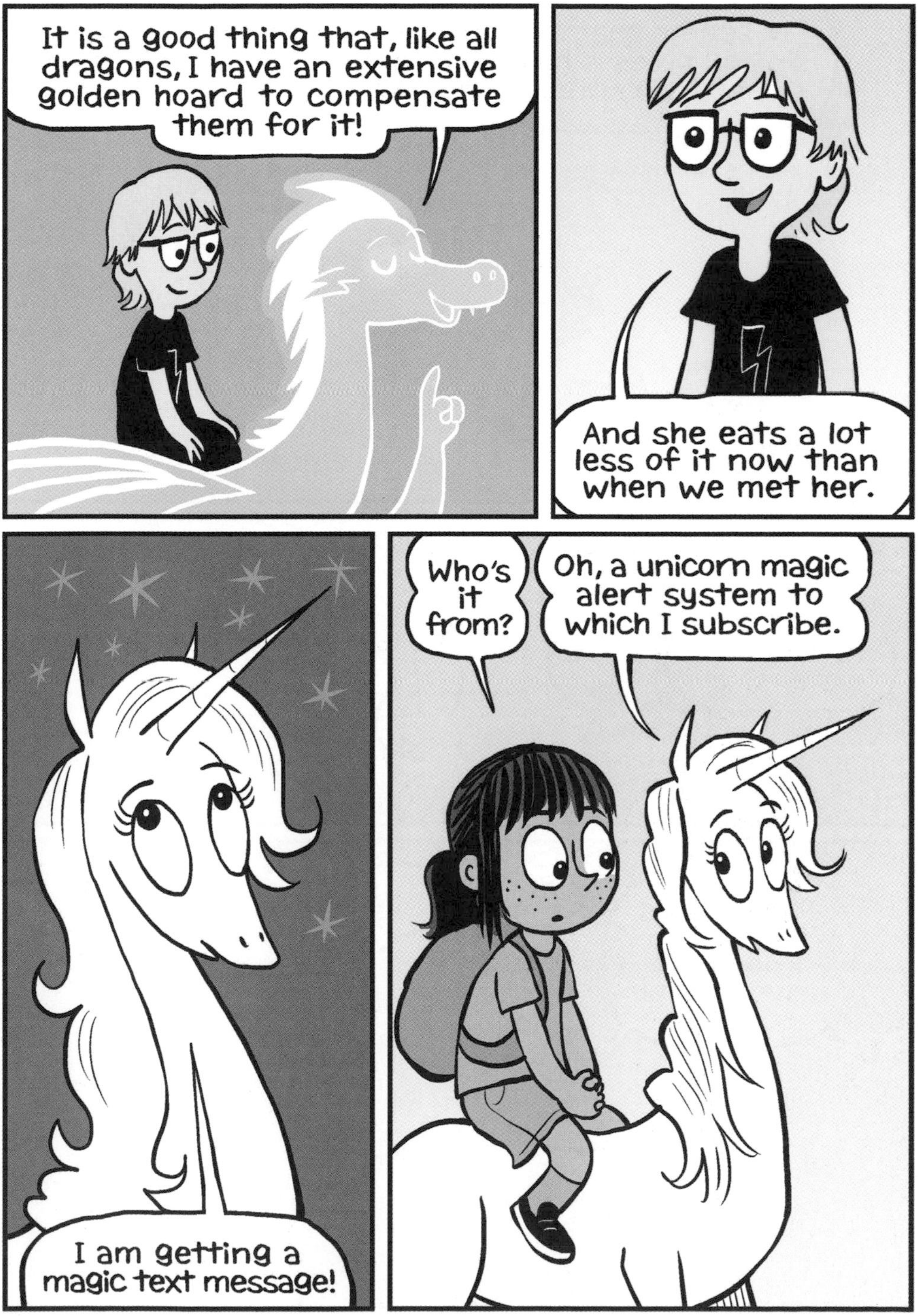
It is a good thing that, like all dragons, I have an extensive golden hoard to compensate them for it!
And she eats a lot less of it now than when we met her.
I am getting a magic text message!
Who's it from?
Oh, a unicorn magic alert system to which I subscribe.

MORE TO EXPLORE! A special section featuring fun facts!

MAX'S GUIDE TO POWER PLANTS

Ever wondered where the electricity in your house comes from? It all starts at a power plant—also called a "power station." Here's how the power gets to you.

Fuel (like coal or natural gas) is burned in a giant **furnace**.

The heat from the furnace flows up into a **boiler**, heating the water pipes until a flow of steam is produced.

The pressure from the passing steam turns the metal blades of the **turbine** wheel. The hot steam is condensed and moved through the **cooling tower** so that it turns back into water and can be reused.

The turbine is attached to a **generator**, which uses the motion from the turbine to make electricity. When the turbine is in motion, the wires inside a magnetic field within the generator turn, creating electricity.

The electricity travels out of the generator through **energy cables** to a nearby **step-up transformer** that boosts the electricity to a very high voltage so it can be carried over long distances.

Tall metal **transmission towers** carry the electricity through energy cables to wherever it's needed.

Once the electricity reaches its destination, it goes through a **step-down transformer** that converts it to a lower voltage that can be used in your home after it passes through underground cables to reach the wall **outlets** in your house.

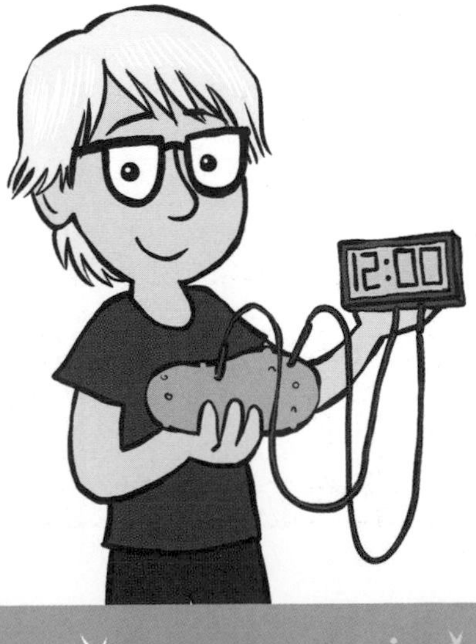
12:00

WHAT ACTUALLY CAUSES POWER OUTAGES?

Are magical storms really to blame when the power goes out? Here's what's behind blackouts:

- **Trees:** If they're not properly pruned, sometimes trees can grow too big or weaken with age, and they interfere with power lines.

- **Storms:** Strong winds, lightning, flooding, and ice can also weaken trees and increases the chances of them falling on electrical equipment. If a storm is strong enough, it can even knock down poles or power lines on its own!

- **Wildlife:** Believe it or not, but dragons only account for a tiny percentage of power outages—other animals such as squirrels, snakes, and birds are more often to blame for damage because they are attracted to the warmth of the electrical equipment or in search of food in electrical substations.

- **Equipment failure:** The electrical grid is very complicated, and sometimes equipment can fail due to age. Other times, equipment fails because it's unable to handle high demand—for example, when everyone in a big city has the air-conditioning on high during an unusually hot summer day.

- **Miscellaneous damage:** What happens if a car crashes into a utility pole? Or what if construction equipment damages power lines? There are many other unusual ways in which the electrical grid can be damaged.

DRINKABLE BLUE LIGHTNING

The drink of dragons! You'll need a black light to experience the full effect of this electrifying drink. The secret is the quinine found in tonic water, which glows in the dark when exposed to a black light.

INGREDIENTS:

water
tonic water, regular or diet
powdered lemonade drink mix

Fill ⅓ of your glass with water, and fill the rest of the glass with tonic water. Add powdered lemonade to taste and mix it well. Then turn out the lights, flip on your black light, and enjoy the zinging, bubbly power of blue lightning in a glass.

WATER-BENDING MAGIC TRICK

You'll think you're wielding magic with this science experiment that relies on static electricity. Shock your friends with a trick that they'll have to see to believe.

TOOLS YOU NEED

nylon comb
water tap (such as the faucet in your kitchen sink)

INSTRUCTIONS

1 Slowly turn on the water tap until you get a small stream of water—the smaller the better, as long as it's a complete stream and not a trickle of drops.

2 Run the comb through your dry hair at least fifteen times. This will charge the plastic with static electricity.

3 Move the comb toward the stream of water without touching it. Go slowly, and behold the power of static electricity!

Without magic, the world feels very strange.

GLOSSARY

ambient (am-bee-ent): pg. 29 – adjective / relating to the immediate surroundings; usually used to describe things like light, temperature, sound, etc.

capacitor (ca-pass-it-ter): pg. 139 – noun / a device used to store electrical energy

golden hoard (gold-en hord): pg. 149 – noun / a huge collection of gold that's been stored somewhere, usually hidden away

gravitate (grav-i-tate): pg. 104 – verb / to move toward something as if pulled by an unseen force

inconspicuous (in-con-spic-u-us): pg. 58 – adjective / not immediately noticeable

locksmith (lock-smith): pg. 108 – noun / a person who makes or repairs locks

matriarchal (may-tree-ark-al): pg. 104 – adjective / describing a society in which women are the leaders

mortgaging (mort-gij-ing): pg. 43 – verb / give someone legal claim to a piece of property you own in exchange for money to be paid back over time

ominously (om-in-nus-lee): pg. 8 – adverb / happening in a way that suggests something bad is going to happen

relevant (rel-lev-vent): pg. 108 – adjective / closely connected to what is being done or considered

singularly (sin-gew-lar-lee): pg. 116 – adjective / in a remarkable or extraordinary way

substations (sub-stay-shuns): pg. 89 – noun / secondary power stations where electric current is transformed so that it can be supplied to customers

uncouth (un-cooth): pg. 78 – adjective / lacking polish or grace

Andrews McMeel Publishing
a division of Andrews McMeel Universal
1130 Walnut Street, Kansas City, Missouri 64106

www.andrewsmcmeel.com

19 20 21 22 23 SDB 10 9 8 7 6 5 4

ISBN: 978-1-4494-8359-3

Library of Congress Control Number: 2017931089

Made by:
Shenzhen Donnelley Printing Company Ltd.
Address and location of manufacturer:
No. 47, Wuhe Nan Road, Bantian Ind. Zone,
Shenzhen China, 518129
4th Printing—4/15/19

ATTENTION: SCHOOLS AND BUSINESSES

Andrews McMeel books are available at quantity discounts with bulk purchase for educational, business, or sales promotional use. For information, please e-mail the Andrews McMeel Publishing Special Sales Department: specialsales@amuniversal.com.

Check out more *Phoebe and Her Unicorn*

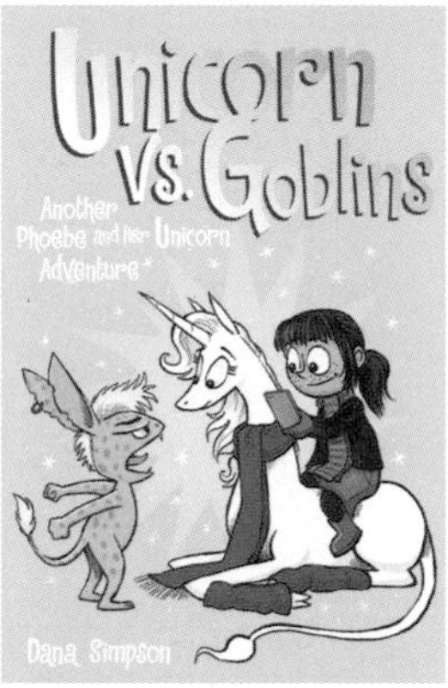
Unicorn vs. Goblins
Another Phoebe and Her Unicorn Adventure
Dana Simpson

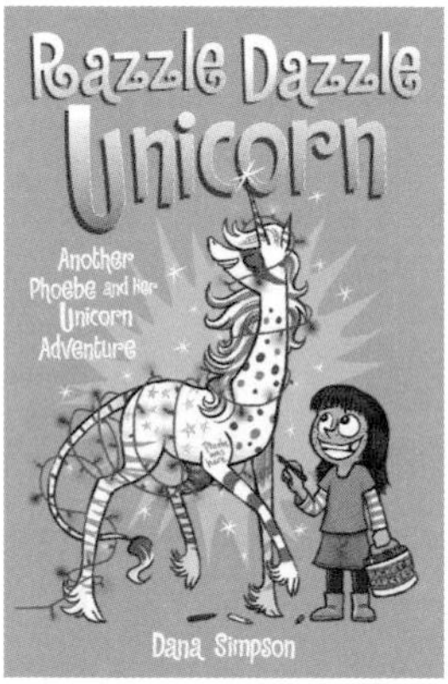
Razzle Dazzle Unicorn
Another Phoebe and Her Unicorn Adventure
Dana Simpson

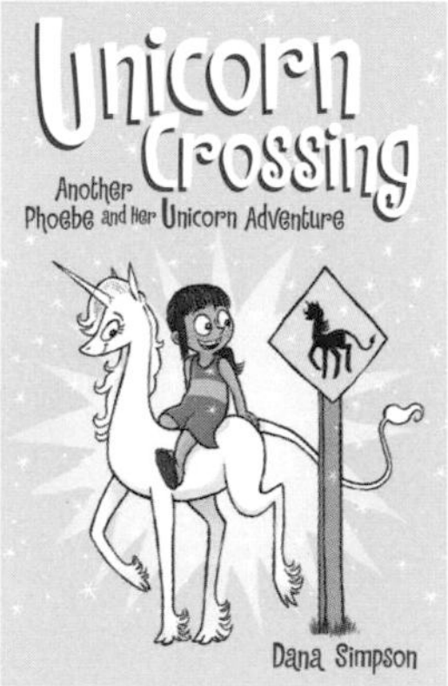
Unicorn Crossing
Another Phoebe and Her Unicorn Adventure
Dana Simpson

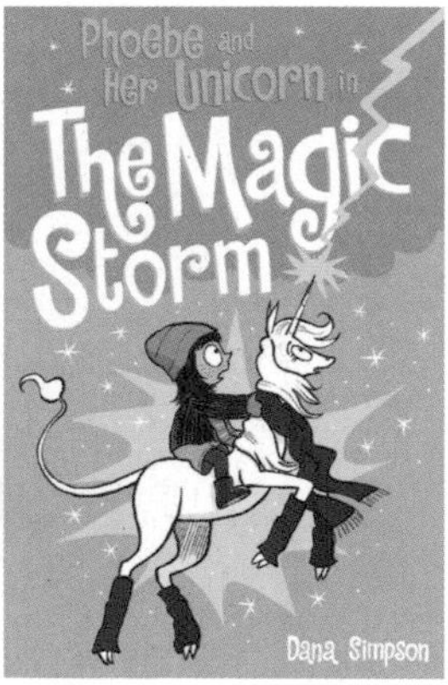
Phoebe and Her Unicorn in
The Magic Storm
Dana Simpson

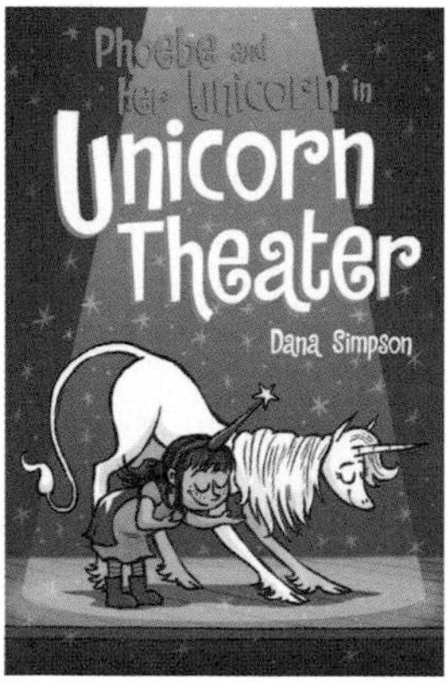
Phoebe and Her Unicorn in
Unicorn Theater
Dana Simpson

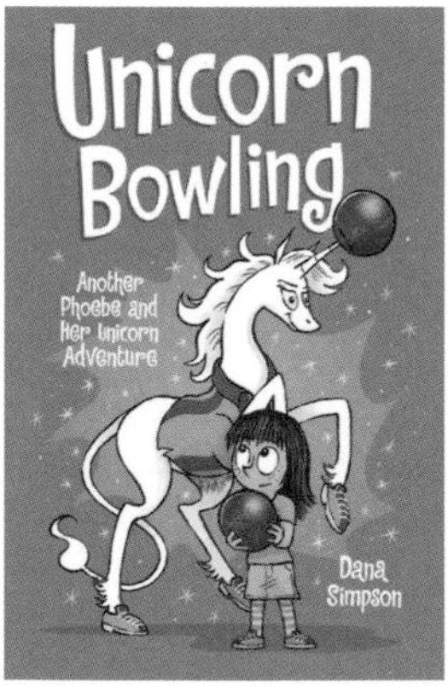
Unicorn Bowling
Another Phoebe and Her Unicorn Adventure
Dana Simpson

If you like Phoebe, look for these books!

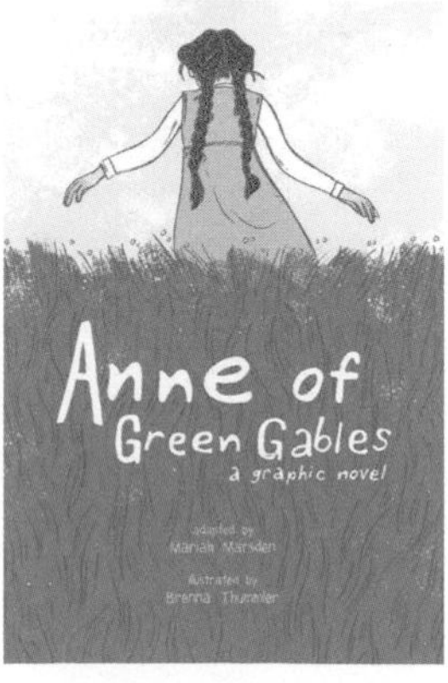
Anne of Green Gables
a graphic novel

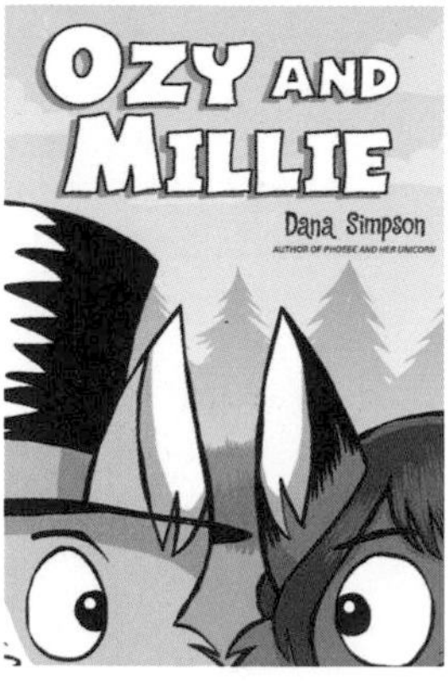
OZY AND MILLIE
Dana Simpson
AUTHOR OF PHOEBE AND HER UNICORN

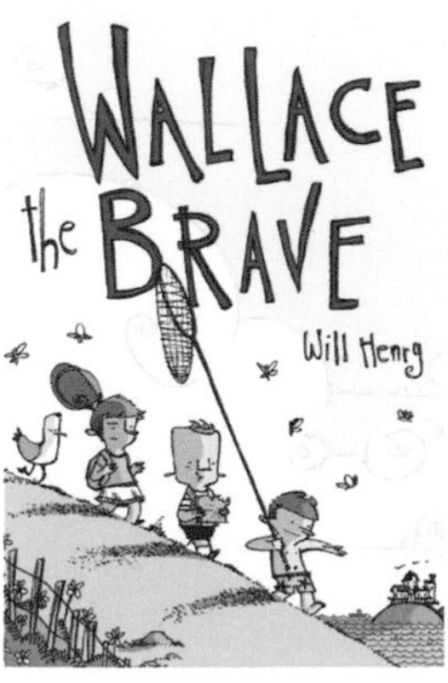
WALLACE the BRAVE
Will Henry